Max shifted closer still. "_____ incredibly beautiful."

I couldn't help it—my heart warmed at the compliment. It beat more deeply, slowly, thudding inside my chest and echoing in my ears.

I told myself to hang on to reality. But _myself_ didn't want to do that right now.

Max touched my arm. The touch was simple. It was light. His thumb brushed slowly across my skin, and I lit up like one of the mesquite trees. Logic and reason flew into the night.

"Max," I whispered.

"Layla," he whispered back.

The breezed cocooned us as he stepped in. His hand slid to my bare shoulder. His other touched the small of my back.

I put my palms on his chest, thinking to stop him, thinking they'd be a barrier between us that would pull me out of this spell.

But it didn't work out that way.

* * *

The Twin Switch by Barbara Dunlop is part of the Gambling Men series.

Dear Reader,

Welcome to *The Twin Switch*, book one of the Gambling Men series. Despite its title, the series is a celebration of girlfriends, best friends and lifelong friends.

I was lucky enough to grow up with an amazing group of girls all living on the same block. From the time we were toddlers to today, where we have careers and grown children, our bonds and roots have run deep. Over the years, we've supported each other through triumphs and trials, both big and small.

In *The Twin Switch*, Layla Gillen follows her lifelong friend and soon-to-be sister-in-law, Brooklyn Christie, to Vegas, where Layla finds herself caught between loyalty to her brother and an attraction to the sexy Max Kendrick—twin brother of the man trying to steal Brooklyn away.

I hope you enjoy the story!

Barbara

BARBARA DUNLOP

———

THE TWIN SWITCH

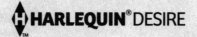

HARLEQUIN® DESIRE

Recycling programs
for this product may
not exist in your area.

ISBN-13: 978-1-335-20886-6

The Twin Switch

Copyright © 2020 by Barbara Dunlop

Printed in U.S.A.

www.Harlequin.com

New York Times and *USA TODAY* bestselling author **Barbara Dunlop** has written more than forty novels for Harlequin, including the acclaimed Chicago Sons series for Harlequin Desire. Her sexy, lighthearted stories regularly hit bestseller lists. Barbara is a three-time finalist for the Romance Writers of America's RITA® Award.

Books by Barbara Dunlop

Harlequin Desire

Chicago Sons

Sex, Lies and the CEO
Seduced by the CEO
A Bargain with the Boss
His Stolen Bride

Whiskey Bay Brides

From Temptation to Twins
Twelve Nights of Temptation
His Temptation, Her Secret

Gambling Men

The Twin Switch

Visit her Author Profile page at Harlequin.com, or barbaradunlop.com, for more titles.

You can also find Barbara Dunlop on Facebook, along with other Harlequin Desire authors, at Facebook.com/harlequindesireauthors.

For Susie Ross:

Thanks for the inspiration!

One

If I could choose my own sister, it would be Brooklyn.

She made me laugh.

Better still, she made me think. And when things went bad, which they often did, she'd lie down beside me on my blue silk comforter and listen for hours. She knew when the fix was ice cream and when it was tequila.

She was smart, too. She got straight A's right from elementary school.

Me, I was more of a B-plus person. But I was a pretty good listener. And I could twist a mean French braid, which Brooklyn liked.

She had long blond hair and beautiful blue eyes. She tanned, too. We both tanned.

Since we were little kids, we'd spent our summers at the beach on Lake Washington. First it was the swings and the jungle gym. A little older, we'd race to the floater in the middle of the swimming area, dive off, then dry on our towels in the sun. Older still, we hung out at the snack bar, batting our lashes at cute boys and getting them to buy us milkshakes.

I didn't get to choose my own sister. But it was happening, anyway.

In just two weeks, Brooklyn was marrying my big brother, James.

"I can see the Golden Gate Bridge," Sophie Crush said from the front seat of the cab.

I was in the middle of the back seat squished between Brooklyn and Nat Remington. That's what happened when you insisted on taking a hybrid from the airport.

"Do you think we'll have views from our rooms?" Nat asked.

"I want a view of the spa," Brooklyn said. "From inside the spa, I mean."

"You heard the bride," I said.

I flexed my shoulders in anticipation of a deep stone massage. I'd had one once before. It had been a little slice of Heaven that I was dying to repeat.

"Pedicures," Sophie said.

"Facials," Nat said.

"I want to sit in the sauna," Brooklyn said.

"I feel my pores opening up already," I said.

The sauna sounded like a great idea. So did a facial. I was the maid of honor, and I was determined to look my best.

Unlike some brides—more selfish brides—Brooklyn had chosen gorgeous bridesmaid dresses. They were airy and knee length with strapless sweetheart necklines and fitted bodices of azure-blue chiffon that faded to pale sky at the hemline.

My auburn hair was tricky but, happily, the colors worked. Because for a single twenty-six-year-old, a wedding was a really good place to meet new guys.

I was at a disadvantage this time since half the guests would be my own relatives. Plus I'd met nearly all of Brooklyn's friends and family over the years. Still, she might have an undiscovered hot second cousin or two in

BARBARA DUNLOP 9

the right age range. A woman could never discount an opportunity.

The cab pulled to a halt beside a rotating glass door and miles of windows that looked into the lobby. Stylized gold lettering spelled out The Archway Hotel and Spa on a marble pillar.

Three men in crisp steel-gray short-sleeved jackets simultaneously opened our doors.

"Welcome to the Archway," one of them said to Brooklyn, his gaze lingering on her sea-breeze eyes before moving past her to me.

His smile was friendly. He was cute, but I wasn't about to get interested.

Not that I have anything against valets. He could be putting himself through grad school for all I knew. Or maybe he liked living near the beach and having flexible hours.

Brooklyn moved past him, and he held out his hand to me.

I took it.

It was strong, slightly calloused, definitely tanned. Maybe he was a surfer.

I'm not a snob about professions. I'm a high school math teacher, and that isn't the most prestigious job. I'm open to meeting people from all walks of life.

He did have really gorgeous hazel eyes, and a strong chin, and a bright white smile.

I came to my feet and he let go of my hand, taking a step back.

"We'll take care of the bags," he said, his gaze holding mine a little longer than normal.

It took me a second to realize he was waiting for a tip.

I almost laughed at myself. He wasn't flirting with me—at least not with any romantic intent. He did this with everyone who arrived at the hotel. It was probably how he paid for his surfboard.

I rustled through my purse for a five and handed it over.

It was a splurging kind of a weekend, I reminded myself. You only got the perfect sister-in-law once in your life.

Two bellhops wheeled our luggage into the lobby and we followed.

"We could go see some male exotic dancers," Nat said.

Brooklyn winced. "Pass."

I smiled. I knew Nat was joking. If Sophie had suggested it, I might have taken her seriously.

"Don't be too hasty," Sophie said. "After all, what do you think James is doing with the guys right now?"

"You think James is watching male exotic dancers?" Brooklyn asked as we made our way past the fountain to the check-in desk.

"Female," Sophie said.

There was no lineup. In fact, there were three attendants available. Nice.

Brooklyn swung her tote bag onto her shoulder. "The guys are watching a doubleheader."

"Afterward," Sophie said.

I couldn't imagine James going to a strip show. He was absolutely not the type.

But Brooklyn got a funny expression on her face, like she thought maybe it was a possibility, even though the idea was ridiculous.

"Are you checking in today?" the woman behind the counter asked us in a chipper voice that said she was delighted to be here to help us.

"We're the Christie party," Nat answered, deftly pulling a copy of the reservation from her bag.

Hanging back, I spoke to Brooklyn in an undertone. "You're not worried about James, are you?"

Brooklyn frowned and gave a noncommittal shrug. Then she moved toward the counter, digging into her bag. "Do you need my credit card?"

"I just need one for check-in," the woman said. "When you check out, you can split the charges if you like."

I repositioned myself so that I was beside Brooklyn.

"He's not going to see a stripper," I whispered, wondering how she could possibly be worried about James's behavior.

James, with a master's degree in economics, who'd landed a job at one of the most conservative consulting firms in Seattle, who only spoke in complete sentences and who guarded his social media accounts as if he had the nuclear launch codes, would not be hanging out at a strip club.

I couldn't imagine him risking someone snapping his picture in a strip club—even if he did want to see naked women. Which he did not, because there wasn't a woman in the country more beautiful than Brooklyn.

Brooklyn was a fashion buyer for a chain of Seattle boutiques. But she could have been a movie star or a supermodel. There was nowhere for James to go but down in the looks department.

"What's wrong?" I asked her.

She turned her head and smiled. "What could possibly be wrong?"

There was something in her eyes. I couldn't quite put my finger on it.

"Did James do something?" I asked her.

"No."

"Are you mad at him?"

"No."

"Then what...?"

"Nothing." Brooklyn smiled again. "He's perfect. James is perfect. And I'm going to book a spa appointment." She reached for the brochure on the countertop.

"I can help with that," the check-in woman said as she handed Nat's credit card back to her.

"Something with aromatherapy," Brooklyn said.

I wasn't one hundred percent convinced by Brooklyn's nonchalance, but I thought about hot stones pressed slowly across my oiled back and decided anything else could wait.

Massaged and steamed and showered and dressed, I spotted Sophie sitting at the bar in the lounge. A jazz trio was playing in the corner while candles flickered on the mottled glass tables. The chairs were white leather, and a glass mosaic decorated the wall behind the bar.

I was wearing three-inch heels with my silver cocktail dress, so I was happy to rest my feet by perching next to Sophie.

"What are you drinking?" I asked.

"Vodka martini."

The bartender arrived, another cute guy. "Can I get you something?"

His smile was friendly, definitely flirtatious. And he was classically handsome, probably thirty or so, with intelligent gray eyes.

I certainly had nothing against bartenders, except when you met them at their work. There they flirted with everybody. Like the valets out front, their shift was made or broken by their tips.

"I'll take one of those," I said, pointing to Sophie's glass.

I smiled at him, but made it brief. I didn't want to spend

the evening chatting with the bartender. I wanted to spend it with my girlfriends.

Across the lounge, a very handsome profile came into my view, distracting me.

Okay, this guy wasn't a bartender, or a valet, or a public school teacher of any kind—that was for sure.

His perfectly cut suit was draped over a perfectly sculpted body. His haircut was shaggy-neat, that kind where you paid the earth to look like you'd rolled out of bed and had every hair fall naturally into place.

Even as I mentally mocked the style, I liked it.

He turned, and I caught his handsome face full-on. He could have just walked off a magazine cover. He should have walked off a magazine cover with that chiseled chin and those startlingly bright blue eyes.

He caught me staring, but he didn't smile. I felt heat hit my cheeks, anyway.

And then it was over. He turned and kept walking like our eyes meeting had never happened. And maybe it hadn't. Maybe he hadn't been staring at me at all. Maybe it was just the fevered musing that took flight in my head when I saw a good-looking guy lately.

I'd read a statistic last month that said sixty-seven percent of women met their husbands before they graduated from college. So I was already in the bottom thirty-three percent.

When you added that to the twenty-one percent of women who never married at all, my odds looked grim. I had a twelve percent chance of meeting Mr. Right.

Don't get me started on the fifty percent divorce rate because that left me at six percent. And six percent was truly demoralizing.

"Earth to Layla," Sophie said.

I gave myself a mental shake. This was a girlfriends' weekend.

"Did Brooklyn come down already?" I asked, focusing on the here and now.

Brooklyn and I were sharing a room, while Sophie and Nat were staying together one floor up. We had ended up with a view of the bridge, while they looked into the building next door. We'd offered to trade, but nobody seemed to care about the view.

The rooms had enormous soaker tubs, steam showers and beds that felt like you were floating on a cloud. Nothing else much mattered.

"I haven't seen her yet," Sophie said.

I glanced around but didn't see her, either. "I have eight pillows," I said to Sophie.

"You counted?"

"I counted."

"Did you take the square root?" she asked, grinning as she bit the olive off her blue plastic skewer.

"If I include the gold throw pillow, the square root is three. I considered applying the quadratic formula, but—"

"Layla." It was Brooklyn's happy voice in my ear and I felt her arm go around my shoulders. "I thought you'd never get out of the shower."

"It's a great shower." There was something sensual and indulgent about endless hot water.

"What are you drinking?" Brooklyn sounded overly cheerful.

"Vodka martini," Sophie said. "You?"

"I had a Sunburst Bramble across the lobby there. I wouldn't recommend it."

She wore a short, mauve halter dress with a full skirt that swirled around her toned thighs. Her ankle-high gladiator heels were mottled purple and silver. As always, she looked trendy and stylish.

The bartender seemed to magically appear. "The Sunburst Bramble wasn't to your taste?" he asked Brooklyn, obviously having overheard her comment. "Would you like me to replace it with something else?"

"Would you?" Brooklyn responded. "That's so sweet of you."

He slid a slim, leather-bound cocktail menu in front of her.

"Why don't you pick," she said, sliding it back with a swish of her shoulder-length blond hair. "Something sweeter, maybe with strawberries or a little Irish Mist?"

I did a mental eye roll. This was the Brooklyn who'd gotten us free milkshakes at the beach all summer long. Only that Brooklyn hadn't been engaged to be married.

"How many drinks have you had?" I asked her, wondering if she'd hit the minibar while I was in the shower.

"Just the one. But I'm about to have another."

I told myself to quit worrying. She was in a good mood, and that was great. This was her weekend, after all. I didn't know why I was borrowing trouble.

The bartender brought me my drink.

"I'm off to the ladies'," Brooklyn said. "When my drink comes save it for me."

I turned my head to call after her. "Will do."

I saw three different men follow Brooklyn's progress as she walked to the lobby. It was always that way with her. I wasn't sure she even noticed anymore.

"I think Nat really wants to see exotic dancers," Sophie said to me.

I refocused my attention on Sophie. "No way."

Nat was the most straitlaced of the four of us. She was James, only in female form. She was literally a librarian.

"I think she might be ready to burst out of that shell."

"That would be entertaining," I said, thinking it really would.

Nat's long-term boyfriend had split with her a few months back. I knew she hadn't dated anyone since. I also knew Henry had been hard on her self-esteem.

Sure, Nat wore glasses. But they were cute glasses, and she had the sweetest spray of freckles across her cheeks. Her brown hair might not be the most exotic of shades, and she wasn't glam like Brooklyn, but she had the most beautiful smile that lit up her pale blue eyes.

"She's chatting up a guy right now." Sophie inclined her head.

I turned to surreptitiously follow Sophie's gaze.

Sure enough, Nat was at a corner table, head leaned in talking to a guy in a nicely cut suit jacket and an open-collared white shirt. He looked urbane attractive, but more fine-featured than appealed to me. But then I wasn't Nat.

Something banged above us.

I reflexively ducked as my adrenaline surged.

The room suddenly turned black, garnering audible gasps and a few high-pitched shrieks from the crowd.

It went quiet.

"Whoa." I blinked to focus.

"What was that?" Sophie asked into the darkness.

"Something broke."

"It sure did."

My eyes adjusted, and I could see the candles now, little dots of light on the tables illuminating the faces closest to them. They reflected off the windows. Beyond, across the bay, I could see the lights of ships and sailboats in the distance.

"Nothing but a power failure, folks." It was the bartender's hearty voice. "It happens sometimes. Please sit tight and enjoy the ambience. I'm sure the lights will come back on soon."

"At least we're not waiting on our drinks," Sophie said, lifting her glass to take another sip.

"I wonder if Brooklyn will be able to find us." I looked around, but I couldn't see much of anything beyond the candlelight.

"Hey, guys." Nat appeared and hopped up on the stool next to Sophie.

"What happened to your man?" Sophie asked.

"When the lights went out, he squealed like a little girl."

"That's disappointing," I said.

Sometimes I wondered if there were any good men left in the world. I had a list of qualities. I mean, it wasn't a long list, mostly to do with integrity and temperament. But squealing like a little girl was definitely not on it.

"So not the type to rescue you from a bear," Sophie said to Nat. She sounded disappointed.

There was laughter in Nat's voice. "Who needs rescuing from a bear?"

"I might go camping," Sophie said.

"You?" Nat asked.

Five-star restaurant manager, downtown high-rise-dwelling Sophie was definitely not the outdoor type.

"Well, maybe you," Sophie said.

Nat had been known to spend time outside—at least in her rooftop garden.

"Then that's *definitely* not my guy." Nat took a two-second gaze back over her shoulder.

I realized then, that after a mere five minutes I'd wondered if Nat's guy would be *the* guy. It could have been a really romantic story—Nat meeting the love of her life while spending a girls' weekend in San Francisco celebrating Brooklyn's wedding.

We were all single. Well, Brooklyn wouldn't be single for long. But Sophie, Nat and me hadn't had a lot of luck meeting men.

Good guys were hard to find. I could list the flaws in each of my dates from the past six months: too loud, too nerdy, too intellectual, too moody.

I knew how it sounded. And I realized perfectly well what I was doing with that list. If I focused on the guys, I didn't have to explore the possibility that it was me—which, of course, deep down, I knew it was.

I'd love to live in denial. And I would if I could figure out a way that I didn't know denial was denial.

So far, I hadn't been able to make that work.

"Where's Brooklyn?" Nat asked.

"Ladies' room," I said.

Sophie craned her neck to gaze across the dim room. "She should be back by now. I hope she's not stuck in an elevator."

"I'm going to go look for her." I slid off my bar stool.

"You'll get lost, too," Nat said. "Or you'll trip and break your ankle."

I remembered my black-and-gold sling-back stilettos. They were stylish, but not the most stable footwear in my closet. Nat made a good point.

Instead, I retrieved my phone from my purse and shot Brooklyn a text.

I climbed back up and took a sip of my drink.

We all stared at my phone for a few minutes, but Brooklyn didn't text back.

"Stuck on an elevator," Nat said in conclusion.

"Or in an ambulance," Sophie said. "I bet she was rushing to get back to us in the dark, and it all went bad."

"Don't even joke about that," I said. "There are five hundred people coming to her wedding."

"And it's a long way up the aisle at St. Fidelis's," Nat said. "What if she broke her leg?"

"She didn't break her leg," I said and then realized I was tempting fate. "I mean, I *hope* she didn't break her leg."

Brooklyn with a broken leg would be an unmitigated disaster.

It was thirty minutes before the lights came on. When they did, conversation around us spiked for a moment, and there was a smattering of applause.

The bartender went back to work, and the waitresses began circulating around the room. Brooklyn still hadn't returned from the ladies' room, and I looked at the lobby entrance, trying to spot her.

"There she is," Sophie said.

"Where?" I asked, disappointed in my powers of observation.

"Left side of the lobby. Talking to a guy."

I leaned in for a better angle, but I still couldn't see her.

"It looks like she got more support from random men than I did," Nat said.

"He's hot," Sophie said.

I got down from the bar stool so I could see more of the lobby.

"Whoa," both Sophie and Nat said in unison.

"What?"

I saw a broad hand on Brooklyn's shoulder, and I could almost feel the touch myself. The rest of the man was blocked from view by the lounge wall.

She smiled, and then the hand disappeared.

I surged forward, but whoever he was walked away too fast.

"Seriously?" Sophie said. "The three of us are all single, and *she* ends up with him in the blackout?"

"Fate is cruel," Nat said.

"What did he look like?" I asked.

"Hot," Sophie said.

"Tall," Nat said.

"Tall and hot," Sophie said.

"Thanks for that specific detail," I said.

Brooklyn was coming toward us.

"Who was that?" Nat called to her.

"Can I meet him?" Sophie asked.

"You don't get to call dibs," Nat said.

"Dibs," Sophie said.

Brooklyn was smiling and shaking her head as she drew closer. Her cheeks were flushed, and there was an odd brightness to her eyes.

"What happened?" I asked.

"The power went off," she said.

"Did you get his name?" Sophie asked.

Brooklyn shook her head. "Can't help you with that."

"He squeezed your shoulder," I said.

From my vantage point, the touch seemed intimate. That tanned, strong hand squeezing down on Brooklyn's shoulder had sent a shiver up my own spine.

I tried to imagine how James would feel about someone touching Brooklyn that way. He wouldn't like it. Of that, I was sure.

"He was saying goodbye," Brooklyn said.

"What's wrong with you?" Sophie asked me.

"Who squeezes a strange woman's shoulder?" I asked.

"Who doesn't?" Sophie returned.

"It's not like he kissed me," Brooklyn said.

For some reason, her words didn't make me feel any better.

"He can kiss me," Sophie said.

It suddenly occurred to me that Brooklyn might already know the man. That would explain the touch.

But if that was true, why wasn't she saying so? Was the guy an old boyfriend? Not that she could have an old boyfriend without me knowing. It was impossible.

"We're going to be late for our dinner reservation," Nat said.

"Was my drink ever served?" Brooklyn asked.

"I think it got lost in the excitement," Sophie said.

As if on cue, the bartender arrived. "I think you'll like this one. I call it an icy wave."

The drink was in a tall glass, blue green in color, with lots of crushed ice and a strawberry garnish.

"Thank you," Brooklyn said to him.

He waited while she took a sip.

I waited impatiently to ask her another question.

"It's good," she said.

The bartender beamed.

Before I could speak up, shaggy-neat-hair guy walked back into the lounge. The sight of him sent a jolt of electricity across my chest. I sucked in a breath.

He seemed to hear me, or maybe he just felt me staring, because he turned, and we locked gazes. This time there was no mistaking it.

His mouth crooked into a half smile. I couldn't tell if he was greeting me or mocking me. It could be that my lust was obvious to him even at this distance.

No, not lust, I told myself. Lust made my reaction sound salacious.

This was interest, no more, no less. And there was nothing wrong with being interested in a good-looking guy across the bar.

"We have a reservation in the Moonside Room," Nat said, interrupting my musings.

I forced myself to break the gaze.

And I was absurdly proud of breaking off the look first this time. I found myself smiling in satisfaction. I had to resist the urge to check shaggy-neat-hair guy's reaction to my shift in attention.

"I can have your drink brought up to the restaurant for you," the bartender said to Brooklyn.

No mention of my drink, or Sophie's. But then that was the way of the world.

"Thank you so much." Brooklyn flashed her friendly blue eyes.

"Not a problem."

I could tell the bartender thought he had a shot—despite the big diamond ring on Brooklyn's left hand. She had a knack for that—for doing nothing in a way that ever so subtly led men on.

Sophie was very pretty. Nat was girl-next-door cute. But none of us could hold a candle to Brooklyn's allure. Men tripped over their own feet when she was in the room. She invariably got us great tables and great service from earnest waiters and maître d's.

Mostly I just took the perks without bothering to be jealous of Brooklyn.

"Through the lobby?" she asked the bartender.

"Straight across to the gold elevator. It will take you to the fifty-eighth floor. Mandy can show you." He beckoned one of the waitresses.

"Just in case we can't read the sign," Nat whispered to me.

"Just in case he misunderstood the diamond ring," I whispered back.

"Men have no consciences."

"Luckily for James, Brooklyn does."

My best friend, and an only child with two distant,

busy parents, Brooklyn had spent countless weekends and holidays with my big extended family. She'd had a crush on James since we were old enough to know what a crush was. He'd finally invited her to the junior prom, and there'd been no going back.

Their relationship made such perfect sense for everyone, including me. I'd been testing the term *sister-in-law* inside my head for months now. I couldn't wait to use it in real life.

As we walked to the elevator, I looked around for shaggy-neat-hair guy.

He wasn't in the bar, and he wasn't in the lobby.

Ah, well. There was always tomorrow.

The sauna and spa lounge were coed. He could be a spa guy.

Or maybe I'd check out the exercise room. He definitely looked like the weight-training type. And I could see him on an elliptical machine…or rowing.

I could definitely picture him rowing.

Two

I wasn't a morning person at the best of times.

It was doubly hard to wake up with the daylight filtered by an opaque blind, the air in the room cool on my face and cozy in a bed that was softer than a cloud.

Reluctantly giving up my state of sleep, I reached for the last wispy threads of my dream. There'd been a blue-eyed man on a surfboard off the beach of a tropical island. A dog was playing in the sand while the palm-frond room of a nearby hut rustled in the floral breeze.

I'd felt safe and warm inside the hut, but I couldn't remember why. I struggled to find the details, but the synaptic connections evaporated, locking me out of my subconscious.

It was morning.

I opened my eyes to see the bathroom light on, the door partially closed.

I listened, hoping Brooklyn would be done soon so I could take a turn.

I looked to the bedside clock and found it was nearly nine.

I'd slept a long time.

I was hungry.

As I waited for Brooklyn, I weighted the cost-benefit

of eggs Benedict. It was my all-time favorite breakfast. But the béarnaise sauce meant extra crunches next week and maybe some extra laps in the pool.

My bridesmaid dress was exactly the right size, and too much indulgence this weekend would blow the lines. A custom-fit dress deserved the flattest stomach I could muster.

Still, one breakfast of eggs Benedict—how much would that hurt?

"Brooklyn?" I called out. "Are you almost done?"

My bladder capacity wasn't unlimited.

She didn't answer, and I got up out of bed.

We'd come back to the room together after dinner last night.

While we ate, she'd been alternately chipper and chatty, and then suddenly lost in thought. She was the first of my close friends to get married, so I couldn't tell if this was normal. It could easily be normal, but something seemed off.

I'd planned to talk to her once we got in bed. There was nothing like girl talk in the dark to get to the heart of a matter.

But I'd gone out like a light while she was still in the bathroom.

Now, I found it empty.

I was both surprised and relieved. I wouldn't have to wait any longer, but I did wonder why she didn't wake me up for breakfast.

I hoped they all hadn't eaten without me. I'd be more willing to dive into a plate of eggs Benedict if I had co-conspirators in the indulgence. Hey, if the bride was going all out, I wasn't going to be a wet blanket.

I changed quickly, ignoring my makeup bag, and threw my hair into a ponytail. I climbed into a pair of jeans and a casual blue blouse along with a pair of ankle boots and some earrings. I was good enough for breakfast.

I headed for the Sunriser dining room on the main floor.

There I found Sophie and Nat. Like me, they'd decided it was a day to go for it with plates of gooey Belgian waffles and steaming mugs of hot chocolate.

"Where's Brooklyn?" I asked as I sat down on a cushioned seat at the table for four.

The room was West Coast elegant, with gleaming wood beams soaring above us and a high wall of windows looking onto the bay. Sunlight streamed in across leafy plants and navy-colored tablecloths, glinting off the glassware and silver.

"We thought she was with you," Sophie said.

"She wasn't in the room when I woke up."

The waitress offered me coffee, and I gratefully accepted, finding the cream in a little silver pitcher in the middle of the table.

"Did you check the spa?" Nat asked.

"No. Don't you think it's too early?"

"She's probably working out," Nat said. "Her wedding dress doesn't leave any room for error."

I found myself rethinking my eggs Benedict.

Nat cut into her waffle, releasing a wave of the delicious aroma.

"Are you ready to order?" the waitress asked me.

"Eggs Benedict," my mouth said before my brain could mount a decent argument against it.

Once made, I was happy with the decision. I could work out at the hotel gym sometime today. It was going to be worth it.

"The woman has willpower," Sophie said of Brooklyn.

I smiled at that as I sipped my sweetened coffee. It was true.

Thanks to Brooklyn's insistence, we swam to the far floater and back every time we drank a milkshake at the Lake Washington Beach. I didn't gain an ounce over summer breaks. To this day, I used swimming to stay in shape.

I should thank her for that.

I'd have plenty of time in the future.

She and James were shopping for houses in Wallingford. The area was close to my apartment in Fremont. After the wedding, we'd be able to see each other even more often than we did now.

While I waited for my breakfast, I shot her a text.

"At least we know she's not stuck in an elevator this time," Nat said.

"Are we shopping this morning?" Sophie asked.

"Do you need something?" I glanced at my phone, but there was no symbol to indicate Brooklyn was answering.

"Clothes," Sophie said. "Maybe some throw pillows or shelves. I could use some shelves for that little corner by the patio door. I bought those two blown-glass sculptures at the pier last month, and I have nowhere to put them."

"I don't need anything," Nat said.

"I respectfully disagree," Sophie said. "Your studio needs a complete makeover."

"It's functional," Nat said with a sniff.

"It's criminal," Sophie said. "All that glorious potential, and you haven't done a thing with it."

"I hung some pictures."

"That *I* gave you. On hooks that were on the wall from the last tenant. The arrangement doesn't even make sense." Sophie turned to me. "We should go on a shopping spree for Nat's place."

"We should probably ask Brooklyn," I said, thinking

the weekend was supposed to be all about her. And I'd make it all about her, too, if I could only track her down.

My eggs Benedict arrived, looking outstandingly delicious.

"Brooklyn will go for it. She loves shopping," Sophie said.

I took a first bite. It was to die for.

I'd be happy to shop or sightsee or hit the pool deck. I'd even go for another massage. I'd always go for another massage.

"In that case, we can shop for Brooklyn," Nat said. "I don't want to clutter my place up with knickknacks and dust collectors."

"Another word for them is art." Sophie smirked as she went for her phone. "If the bride says we're redecorating your studio, we're redecorating your studio."

"That's not how it works," Nat said.

"It's exactly how it works." Sophie held her phone to her ear.

"I'm counting on you," Nat said to me. "Talk some sense into her."

"I can't see redecorating your apartment being Brooklyn's first choice," I said honestly.

My money was on Fisherman's Wharf or Golden Gate Park.

"She's not answering," Sophie said.

I hoped that meant Brooklyn was in a shower at the gym. She should really get over here and try some of these eggs.

"What the heck?" Sophie said, surprise in her tone.

I looked up.

She put her phone under my nose with a friend-finding app open. I squinted, but it was too close for me to see the little map.

When she spoke again, she sounded completely baffled. "What's Brooklyn doing back at the airport?"

My first thought was Brooklyn had been kidnapped.

It was the only thing that made sense.

She had no reason to leave the hotel voluntarily. We had spa appointments, and there were Belgian waffles and hot chocolate on the menu. What more could a woman ask for?

I wanted to call the police right away, but Nat convinced me they'd need more evidence before they opened a missing-person case. Brooklyn was an adult, and she hadn't been gone very long by law-enforcement standards.

Nat was right.

I was letting emotion overrule reason. That wasn't like me at all.

Instead, we checked the hotel room and discovered Brooklyn's suitcase was gone.

I took heart from that. I took that to mean she'd left willingly. Our best guess was that there'd been an emergency in the middle of the night—maybe a medical emergency, presumably one of her family members, maybe her mom or dad.

If something had happened to James, they would definitely have called me, too. Still, it made no sense that she wouldn't wake me up. I'd have gone with her.

While I was pondering the mystery, I came across her note.

I opened my mouth to alert Sophie and Nat. But then I read it and my heart sank to my toes.

I didn't say a thing. Instead, I hid the damning words in my jeans pocket.

"She's off-line," Sophie said, holding out her phone on the friend-finding app.

Brooklyn's icon had disappeared.

"Did she get on a plane to Seattle?" Nat asked.

"Possibly," I said.

"Should we go after her?" Sophie asked.

We should. We would. At least I would.

But I was going by myself. I didn't know much, but I knew Brooklyn hadn't gone back to Seattle.

"We don't know for sure where she went," I said. "Let's not all rush off." There, that sure sounded more like rational me.

It took me a few precious minutes, but I convinced Sophie and Nat to sit tight at the hotel, promising to track down Brooklyn and bring her back to San Francisco to finish off the weekend.

As I made my way to the airport, the note weighed heavy in my pocket.

Layla, it had said. *I'm more sorry than you can know. I've tried so hard, but I can't marry James. I've met my soul mate. Please forgive me.*

Her soul mate? What was she talking about, her soul mate?

James was her soul mate. He was the love of her life. They were fantastic together.

Sitting on a hard, plastic chair in the airport, staring at the departure board, I hunted through my phone and looked up the airspeeds of commuter jets, considering the radius of the distance Brooklyn could have traveled by now, and mapping out the cities in the circle: Sacramento, Reno, Los Angeles.

I rehearsed the many ways I could talk some sense into her.

It had to be temporary insanity—the stress of a five-hundred-guest wedding, or her mother fussing over the dresses and the flowers and the dinner. Or maybe it was James wanting children right away.

I knew Brooklyn wanted to wait a couple of years before they had kids. I didn't think the disagreement had been a deal breaker. But what did I know?

I knew I was going to find out.

I knew that much.

I thought about phoning James. But I couldn't exactly call him out of the blue and ask about his future kids. Plus, he'd want to talk to Brooklyn. I'd have to say she wasn't with me.

He'd try to call her, and who knew where that would lead. Nowhere good, that was for sure.

The marker for Brooklyn's phone suddenly appeared on my screen.

My heart jumped. I'd found her!

She was in Las Vegas.

I was on my feet and heading for the bank of check-in counters while I scrolled to see which airline had the next flight to McCarran Airport.

A few more searches on my phone, a plane ride and an Uber ride later, and I was in the lobby of the Canterbury Sands Hotel.

Brooklyn's phone told me she was here. Since I wasn't with NASA or the CIA, the accuracy of the app was spotty, and I couldn't pinpoint her, but she was definitely here somewhere.

I glanced around. The hotel lobby was posh luxury as far as the eye could see: marble columns, carved woodwork, potted palms, discrete lighting and leather armchairs set into corners and alcoves.

Since she wasn't conveniently hanging around in the lobby, I tried the front desk. Brooklyn wasn't registered. Or maybe she *was* registered, but the professional staff knew better than to reveal personal information about their guests.

I tried explaining I was Brooklyn's maid of honor and we were getting ready for a wedding. But the female desk clerk seemed unimpressed.

I supposed a wedding in Vegas was hardly a monumental event. I'd seen a bride in a limo as my Uber had turned into the hotel drive and another was visible right now posing for photos outside in the garden.

This bride looked gorgeous, and her groom looked happy, as he joked and jostled with his friends. I loved weddings. Who didn't love weddings?

When the bridal party moved on, and Brooklyn still wasn't anywhere in sight, I found an empty table in a lounge at the side of the lobby. I was going to wait it out. Odds were she'd pass by this central point sometime.

I'd tried calling her again, but she hadn't answered. I wasn't about to let her know I was in Vegas. I didn't think she'd run from me again, but it was possible.

I decided it was better to confront her in person. I wanted to see her expression when I asked what I had to ask—which was what *the heck* did she think she was doing?

It was hot, and I was thirsty, so I ordered a five-dollar cola. I was hungry, too, since I hadn't had a chance to finish my divine eggs Benedict. But I couldn't bring myself to order a twenty-five-dollar snack.

This might be a weekend of indulgence, but I had limits. I'd seen the waiter pass by with the order for another table. They served designer food here. Three shrimps and a swirl of greenery weren't going to impact my hunger in any meaningful way. So why waste the money?

I'd texted Nat before the plane took off, so they knew I was on Brooklyn's trail. I kept the soul mate thing—which struck me as a temporary thing—to myself for now. Instead, I let them assume Brooklyn was blowing off steam in the run-up to the wedding.

She was, in a way. Just not in a good way.

Halfway through my glass of cola, my attention caught on a man on the other side of the lounge. He rose and was moving in my general direction. He stopped at one table and chatted, then he stopped at another, and then he waved to a third.

I'm admittedly not the best at facial recognition. Every September I have to make a seating chart for each class and then work really hard to memorize the students' faces. But even with my limited skill, and at this distance, I could swear this was shaggy-neat-hair guy from San Francisco.

I squinted in the dim lounge light, watching him walk and talk and smile.

Then he looked me straight in the eyes, and my chest jolted with that same electricity. Either this was him, or I was a huge sucker for a particular type.

He was coming straight toward me now. Then again, I was sitting near the exit. I told myself not to get too excited. But when it came to good-looking, possibly eligible men, myself didn't listen much.

My brain started to hum. I should keep eye contact. I should smile. I should say something.

"Hello," he said, slowing to a halt next to my table.

"Hi."

A beat went past in silence.

I started to break it. "Were you by any chance—"

I stopped, distrusting my own memory and not wanting to look foolish. Then I told myself to speak up. That was what I told my students. If you have a question, speak up. There are no stupid questions.

"Were you by any chance just in San Francisco?" It did sound foolish when I said it out loud. Worse, it sounded like a line. I might as well have said: "Do you come here often?"

Sweat instantly gathered at my hairline.

"The Archway?" he asked.

Relief rushed through me. I wasn't imagining things. "Yes."

"I thought I recognized you."

My embarrassment disappeared, but my hormones zipped off like a rocket ship. Up close, he was a hunk, superbuff, great-looking, oozing sensuality.

"Business or pleasure?" he asked in a gravelly voice that seemed to come straight from his deep chest.

It was neither, but I wasn't about to go into detail.

"Pleasure," I said.

He swung his gaze around the lounge. "Are you here alone?"

"Yes." I hadn't found Brooklyn yet, so I was currently alone.

He smiled at that. "I'm Max Kendrick." He looked at my drink. "Would you like something more interesting than cola?"

I almost said no. I wasn't here to get picked up in a bar. Then again, this was far from a honky-tonk. It was a fancy hotel lobby. And hadn't I been fantasizing about this very thing just yesterday—meeting a great guy on my gals' weekend?

This one seemed pretty seriously great, and he was dropping right into my lap, and I was sitting here tongue-tied and questioning every breath I sucked into my lungs. I had to get a grip.

"Have you seen the price list?" I don't know why that silly question popped into my head. If he was staying here, and if he was offering, he must be able to afford the prices.

His smile broadened. "A time or two."

"Sure," I said, before I could come up with anything more senseless to blurt out.

"Great." He sat down at the table. "What's your pleasure?"

I considered pulling a Brooklyn by asking him to choose something for me, maybe batting my eyelashes and pretending to be überfeminine.

But überfeminine wasn't me. Neither was batting my eyelashes, or pretending I didn't know my own mind.

"A chardonnay."

"Any preference on the label?"

"No preference." Whatever the house served was going to be fine with me. Given what I'd seen so far of *the house*, I was betting their wine would be spectacular.

He gave the waitress a glance, and she came straight over.

"Can you bring us a bottle of the Crepe Falls Reserve?"

"Right away," she said.

"A bottle?" I asked, wondering if he was less of a gentleman than I'd guessed. Was he expecting me to knock back a few this early in the afternoon?

"Better value that way."

"So you're not trying to get me drunk?"

"Do you have a reason to get drunk? Is everything okay?"

"Everything's fine." The answer was automatic—even though *fine* was quite the stretch at this particular moment.

"Okay," he said, looking suspiciously at my expression. His gaze seemed perceptive.

I had to tell myself he couldn't read my thoughts. "It's all very fine."

"If you say so."

"I do." I took another sweep around the lobby looking

for Brooklyn. I couldn't let her slip past me because I was distracted by Max Kendrick.

"You sure you're not with someone?" he asked.

I gave him a look of reproach. "I'm sure."

"You're jumpy," he said.

"You're suspicious."

He shrugged without denying it.

Fair enough, I supposed. We'd only just met.

"I'm watching for someone," I said.

"Who?"

"A friend. A girlfriend. I'm meeting her here and I don't want to miss her."

"That's not exactly alone."

"It is until she gets here."

"You lied."

"I didn't lie."

"You omitted. You're hiding something."

I wasn't about to touch that one. "You thought I was a cheater."

"Maybe."

"Is that a takes-one-to-know-one statement? Do you have a girlfriend? Are you a cheater?"

"Nope."

"How do I know you're not lying? Cheaters probably lie."

His smile said he got that I was joking. I felt warm about that. Not everyone caught on to my sense of humor.

The waitress returned with our wine, and we both fell silent as she poured.

When she left, he held up his glass for a toast. "To honesty and integrity."

"Faith and loyalty." I thought about Brooklyn as I touched my glass to his.

I took a sip. The wine was outstanding—crisp, buttery and light on my tongue.

"Now that we know we're on the same wavelength," he said. "Tell me something about you. Maybe start with your name."

I realized then that he'd introduced himself, but I hadn't.

"It's Layla—Layla Gillen."

"Nice to meet you, Layla Gillen. Will you be in Vegas for long?"

"I certainly hope not."

He quirked an eyebrow. "You have something against Vegas?"

"No, nothing. It's the first time I've been here." I scanned for Brooklyn again. I spotted a blonde woman in the distance, but she turned and I saw her profile—not Brooklyn.

"Where are you from?" Max asked.

I turned my attention back to him. "Seattle. You?"

"I have a place in New York, but I travel quite a bit. What do you do in Seattle?"

I didn't want to sound nerdy. Then again, I sure wasn't about to lie.

"I'm a teacher."

"What grade?"

"High school."

"What subject."

"Math."

His smile said he'd discovered an embarrassing secret.

My pride kicked in. "You have something against mathematics?"

"You don't look like any math teacher I ever had."

"I'm fully qualified."

"I'm not questioning that."

"It sounded like you were."

"No." He cocked his head and his gaze grew warm. "I was thinking if my math teachers looked like you, I'd have enjoyed the subject a whole lot more."

My heart fluttered. It seriously, embarrassingly, fluttered there for a second.

My cheeks grew warm, and I told myself to get a grip, covering the reaction with another sip of wine.

This was obviously a crush-at-first-sight, and I'd never felt anything like it.

I didn't want to check into a 700-dollar-a-night hotel room when I had a perfectly wonderful prepaid room waiting for me back in San Francisco. But evening was falling, and there was still no sign of Brooklyn.

Max had said goodbye after lunch, and I'd left the table pretending I had somewhere to go. I didn't, of course. But I'd found a comfortable seat at the opposite end of the lobby with a good view of the main entrances and exits.

The vibe of the lobby was beginning to change from daytime to evening. I knew if I wanted to continue blending with the crowd, I had to get out of my jeans.

There were shops dotted around the periphery of the lobby. The clothes were very high-end, but I managed to find a little black dress on a sales rack.

I wasn't about to interrupt my surveillance by heading into the fitting room. Luckily, the dress had simple lines and enough stretch that I was confident it would fit. My black ankle boots weren't exactly perfect for the occasion, but I was wearing a silver necklace and dangling earrings, and I could pull my hair up in a messy bun.

I'd do for the evening crowd.

I hated to interrupt my surveillance, but eventually, the need for a restroom break became urgent. In the ladies'

room, I changed in a flash and was back out in the lobby
again with my jeans and blouse folded into the boutique
shopping bag.

"I take it you don't have a room?" It was Max's voice
beside me.

I was embarrassed, like I'd been caught freeloading.

I worked to erase my guilty expression before facing
him. I wasn't freeloading. I was genuinely waiting for a
hotel guest. And, anyway, the lobby was a public space.

"My girlfriend has a—" I turned and my words dried
up.

This afternoon Max had looked good in a dusty blue
shirt under a steel-gray suit. Now he looked fantastic. His
shirt was crisp white. His suit was black, and his tie was
dark burgundy scattered with black flecks.

"A room?" he prompted.

"Are you going to a party?"

"I wouldn't exactly call it a party." He took in my dress.
"What about you? Big plans?"

I didn't have any plans at all beyond staking out the
lobby until Brooklyn arrived. I refused to let myself think
she and her faux soul mate were holed up in a hotel room
together for the night, ordering room service and loung-
ing in a whirlpool tub.

The image was too much for me to wrap my head
around, so I shook it out of my mind.

"You haven't found her," Max stated. He didn't give me
time to answer. "What's really going on, Layla?"

"Nothing."

"Are you a private investigator?"

"No."

As I denied it, I wondered if Max wanted me to be a
private investigator. Private investigator sounded like an

exciting job, better than math teacher. Maybe I should consider switching careers.

"A stalker?" he asked.

"I'm not a stalker." I wasn't—at least not usually. Today, well, I supposed it was debatable.

"Have you tried calling her?"

"What a *great* idea." I wasn't annoyed with Max. I was just generally annoyed, and that put the sarcasm in my voice. "I don't know why I didn't think of it myself."

He didn't seem to take offense. "I'll take that as a yes."

"That's a yes."

He peered at my expression. "Did you have a fight?"

"No."

"Is she with a guy?"

I was trying not to think about that. I wanted to deny it. But I didn't feel like lying outright to Max. I didn't even feel like omitting anymore.

Other patrons milled around us, dressed to the nines, talking and laughing, coming together in groups and lining up at the on-site restaurants.

"I think she might be," I admitted.

"So she ditched you for a man." Max's words weren't a question.

It wasn't what he was thinking. But I couldn't explain the situation without giving away private information, so I just stood there looking like a pathetic fifth wheel abandoned in the hotel lobby.

"Join me for dinner," he said.

It was a mercy date if I'd ever heard of one. No thank you. "I have no intention of crashing your party."

"There's no party. There's just me."

I didn't believe that for a second. "Then why are you dressed like the top of a wedding cake?"

"Because this is a nice hotel, and it's after six."

"I don't believe you."

"You don't have to believe me. Just join me for dinner."

"So you're saying you have *nothing* to do tonight."

A man like that, in a suit like his, in a place like this? Not a chance.

"I'm saying there's nothing I *have* to do tonight."

"But you have options?"

"We all have options. All the time. Right now, you're my first choice."

"Why?"

"I swear, Layla, I have never had this much trouble getting a woman to have dinner with me."

"I can't," I said, even though I wanted to say yes.

A guy like this didn't come along every day—at least not in my life. In my life, a guy like this didn't come along *any* day.

"Why not?"

"I can't risk missing my girlfriend. She'll be through here anytime."

He gave me a look that said I was borderline delusional. "I'm no expert. But it seems like she doesn't want to be found."

Brooklyn might not want to be found, but for everyone's sake, I needed to find her.

"Maybe you should leave it until tomorrow," Max said.

"No." That would be bad. It would be very bad to leave Brooklyn and her faux soul mate alone for the night. I had to find her as soon as possible.

"I'm assuming she's over twenty-one."

"She's twenty-six."

"There you go. She's perfectly capable of making her own decisions."

Technically that was true. But I knew Brooklyn wasn't

thinking straight. Something was wrong, and I had to get
to the bottom of it before she made a life-altering mistake.

"We can eat in the Grill Room," he said. "See that
curved booth right there, the one facing the lobby? I'll
get the hostess to seat us in it."

I gauged the view from the table. It was probably better than the view I had from here. And I was truly starv-
ing at this point.

"It's probably reserved." It looked like a prime spot.

"I'm sure they'll fit us in." He sounded confident in his
ability to get preferential treatment.

"Do you come here often?" I asked. Then I laughed at
myself. "I didn't mean that the way it sounded."

"You weren't going for a cheesy pickup line?"

"No."

"Too bad."

I ignored the flirtatious lilt to his words, refusing to
let myself meet his gaze. It would be all too easy to let
my imagination run away with me. And the last thing I
needed was a further distraction right now.

"I'm a fairly frequent guest," he said.

"My lucky day."

"I was going to say it was mine."

This time I did look at him. I'm not made of stone. His
smile was warm, and his eyes had an inner glow, and my
heart fluttered again.

Before I could sigh or swoon or do anything else ridiculously humiliating, he started across the lobby to the
restaurant entrance.

"Mr. Kendrick." The hostess's greeting was friendly
as we approached.

"Hi, Samantha. Can you put us at the front booth?"

"Of course, sir."

She extracted two leather-bound, gold-embossed menus from below the counter. "Bernard will seat you."

"Hello, Mr. Kendrick," Bernard said. "It's great to have you with us tonight."

Max waited while I slid in one side of the booth, going partway around. I set my purse and shopping bag beside me.

I felt outclassed by the surroundings, and I was grateful to have ditched the jeans.

Max slid in the other side of the booth and matched my position. It was cozy with the high-backed plush seats, a flickering candle, the two of us sitting only a couple of feet apart.

I had an expansive view of the lobby, but the table still felt intimate.

"Can I have the waiter bring you your usual?" Bernard asked Max.

"Please," Max said to Bernard.

To me, he said, "It's a classic martini with a lemon twist."

"Sounds good." It did.

I hoped the drink would take the edge off my worry. Fretting over Brooklyn wasn't going to help me find her any faster. When she showed up, she showed up.

"The drinks will be out right away," Bernard said. "Please let me know if there's anything else you need."

"They really do know you," I said to Max as I took yet another scan of the lobby.

"They do. But they treat all their customers well."

That had certainly been my experience so far.

"This isn't the kind of place where I usually eat," I said.

He moved the glass-encased candle so we had an unobstructed view of each other. "What's the kind of a place where you usually eat?"

"The Rock a Beach," I said. "It's a funky little seafood place on Moiler Bay. They have picnic tables on a covered deck. There's great local beer on tap. You can get fish and chips served on newspaper or a wooden hammer to crack your crab. In the winter, they close it in with plastic sheeting and light a central fireplace. My family loves it."

"It sounds great."

"You wouldn't need a suit."

"It sounds like I'd need a bib."

"Recommended."

We both smiled.

"I'd like to take you there sometime," he said.

I could see it. I could picture that. And it was great. The image was so compelling that it took me a second to realize what he was doing.

He was *good*. And I was a fool for following along like a little puppy dog.

I wasn't usually swayed by emotion like this. I'm usually nothing but rational. I pride myself on it. I drew back, forcibly pulling myself from his spell. "Wow."

"Wow what?"

"That was fast, and not particularly believable."

"I—"

"You're a smooth talker, Max Kendrick. But here's a heads-up for you—what you're after is not what's going to happen."

"That's not where I was going."

"Sure it wasn't." Logic and reason told me that much.

"You're a skeptic, Layla Gillen. I'm simply enjoying our conversation."

I wasn't about to believe that. Guys often took a shot and backed off when you called them out on it.

Then again, he'd vaguely mentioned a second date. He

hadn't suggested skinny-dipping in his hot tub or checking out his hotel suite. Maybe I was too quick to judge.

"Okay," I said. "My mistake."

"No. It was my mistake for letting it come out wrong. Can I back up a couple of minutes and take a do-over?"

He could. I wasn't about to say no when he put it so reasonably. But just in case I really did have his number, I was keeping up my guard.

Three

Just as the chocolate soufflé arrived with Devonshire cream and a whole lot of pomp and circumstance, I spotted Brooklyn. She was crossing the lobby, her long blond hair swinging in a high ponytail. I couldn't see her face, but I recognized her walk, the slant of her shoulders and the oversize green-and-gold earrings she'd bought from a funky little stand at Pier 54.

The soufflé looked magnificent—a molten center, topped with the Devonshire cream, powdered sugar and plump raspberries. I'd gone with a seafood salad for dinner, saving space for an indulgent dessert. But I couldn't let Brooklyn get away.

"I'm sorry," I said to Max, grabbing my purse and shopping bag as I slid from the booth.

The pastry chef and the waitress looked baffled.

"Is something wrong?" Max asked.

I kept my gaze on Brooklyn. She disappeared behind a pillar.

"I'll settle up later," I called back to him, tossing the words over my shoulder as I hurried away.

I felt terrible sticking Max with the bill. I told myself I could drop off some cash at the front desk. They might be sticky about confirming someone was a guest, but surely they'd take an envelope for them.

I also hated to waste the chef's hard work. He'd clearly taken pride in the chocolate soufflé. I also selfishly hated to miss eating it.

That was twice today.

Indulgence karma was not on my side.

I could see now that Brooklyn was alone. Perfect.

The lobby was octagonal with four passageways leading off the four corners. She headed down one of them. I thought it led to the pool, an outdoor restaurant and an atrium garden.

I wanted to call out, but I didn't think she'd hear me. And I was half-afraid she might try to escape. She'd gone to a lot of trouble to stay away from me.

I knew why she'd done that.

I knew that she knew that I knew she didn't really want to do this. And she knew I'd talk her out of it without half trying.

I saw the paradox in my thinking. If she knew all that, she wouldn't be hiding from me. She'd simply admit she was wrong, and I was right, and she'd made a big mistake. But I was always the rational one between us. Brooklyn was emotional, and she could talk herself into peculiar things.

She was still a hundred feet ahead of me when she turned again, disappearing from my sight.

I broke into a trot, then discovered she'd taken a doorway that led to the garden.

I followed on polished brick pathway that wound through lighted shrubbery and towering palm trees. I hurried, but I couldn't see her in front of me. Then the pathway forked.

I stopped to consider my next move.

I could hear voices in one direction, and music and laughter. I could see the lights of a restaurant or a patio lounge.

The other way was quiet, no sound but a burbling brook beneath an arched footbridge.

Brooklyn liked to be where the action was, so I followed the music.

I came to a café called the Triple Palm. It was fresh and lively, with a breeze blowing through. Beech-wood tables and chairs were surrounded by greenery and decorated with lights and candles. A trio of musicians played in one corner, and a few couples danced on the raised floor. This was Brooklyn's kind of place.

I did a methodical search of the tables. Then I checked the bar area. Then I repositioned to see the entire dance floor.

No Brooklyn.

I couldn't believe I'd guessed wrong.

I didn't have any time to waste.

I trotted again. It was hard to trot in the heeled boots, but they were better than pumps or spiked heels. That was for sure.

I made it to the fork and over the footbridge. Things got quieter around me. The music faded into the distance. The lights were fewer and farther between.

I listened hard, but I didn't hear anything. My best guess was that Brooklyn was meeting her new soul mate in a secluded corner to talk or cuddle or kiss.

I couldn't see her having sex in a hotel garden, not when just anybody could happen by and catch her. That wasn't like Brooklyn.

Then again, *this* wasn't like Brooklyn. I realized there was a chance that she'd been having risky outdoor sex with James all this time without telling me.

I groaned out loud and quickly scrubbed that image from my mind.

"Layla?" It was Max.

I heard his footsteps before he appeared around a corner.

I was more than surprised to see him. "How did you find me?"

"I looked."

I gave him an eye roll.

"I saw you turn toward the atrium. There are only so many places you can go at this end of the hotel."

My guilt over cutting out on him came back. "I was going to drop some cash off at the front desk."

"What for?"

"To pay for dinner, of course."

He waved a dismissive hand. "Don't be ridiculous. I invited you."

"That doesn't mean you should get stuck with the bill. I didn't mean to cut out on you."

"You saw her, didn't you?"

I nodded. "But then I lost her."

"Did you check the Triple Palm?"

"She's not there. And she doesn't seem to be here." I glanced around. "Unless she's found a secret corner to hide."

"You did say she was with a guy."

I shook my head. "I know what you're thinking." I refused to let myself think that. "She's not like that."

"You don't know what I'm thinking. And not like what?"

"She's not having sex in a public garden, that's what."

He grinned in a way that said I was amusing him.

"There are other things for men and women to do in a quiet corner of the garden than have sex."

"I know that."

He shifted a little bit closer to me. "This is a very romantic garden."

Lighted mesquite trees towered above us. Small cactuses lined the path, with pink and yellow flowers adding color. The air was sultry sweet along the smooth, winding red-toned path, heavy with moisture and soft on my skin.

"That's not really what I want to hear," I said.

"Why not?"

His gaze captured mine. It was as sultry as the air, dark and deep.

I forgot what I was saying. "What?"

He shifted closer still. "You know, you are incredibly beautiful."

I couldn't help it—my heart warmed at the compliment. It beat more deeply, slowly, thudding inside my chest and echoing in my ears.

I told myself to hang on to reality. But myself didn't want to do that right now.

Max touched my arm. The touch was simple. It was light. His thumb brushed slowly across my skin, and I lit up like one of the mesquite trees. Logic and reason flew into the night.

"Max," I whispered.

"Layla," he whispered back.

The breezed cocooned us as he stepped in. One hand slid to my bare shoulder. His other touched the small of my back.

I put my palms on his chest, thinking to stop him, thinking they'd be a barrier between us that would pull me out of this spell.

But it didn't work out that way.

I touched the crisp fabric of his shirt. I could feel his heat beneath it. His chest was firm, his pecs defined.

I'm not shallow. I know there's more to a man than the

shape of his body. But the particular shape of this particular man's body was doing very strange things to my brain waves.

I lowered my hands, feeling the ridges of his abs. A sudden vision of him naked bloomed in my mind, my fingertips trailing across his glorious frame.

I wanted that. I wanted it more than I'd wanted anything in a very long time.

He enfolded me in an embrace, the solid, strong, definitive hug of a man who'd decided exactly what he wanted. And what he wanted was me. I was torn between amazement and arousal.

I tipped my chin, and his lips touched mine, and my amazement fled. There was no room for anything inside of me except arousal.

His lips were hot, firm, moist, with the perfect amount of pressure.

He tasted like fine wine and smoky dreams.

My lips softened, they parted. I invited him in and his tongue swept mine in an encompassing kiss that sent waves of pleasure all the way to my toes.

My hands started to move. They unbuttoned his shirt. They touched his skin, and he gave a guttural groan.

"This way," he said.

I didn't know what he meant. I didn't care what he meant, just so long as his kisses didn't stop and he let me keep feeling my way to his shoulders.

I figured out what he meant, and it was a good thing.

I couldn't believe his room was this close. But there we were, down a narrow pathway, across a patio and through some French doors.

You really couldn't call it a room.

It was a suite—a presidential suite or a royal suite, or

something with its very own name. I could feel how big it was even in the dim light.

Then Max pulled off his jacket and ripped his way out of his dress shirt. And everything around me disappeared. He was hot with a capital *H*.

Before I could look my fill, he pushed down the strap of my dress. He kissed his way across my bared shoulder. Every brush of his lips sent new tingles deep into my skin.

I breathed deeply—such a fresh crisp scent. My fingertips traced their way from his abs, to his pecs, up the breadth of his shoulders that went on and on. My lips followed suit, and I felt his warm breath on my hair.

I knew I should stop. My left brain told me I couldn't careen off on a wave of feeling. I had things to do. I had Brooklyn to find.

Finally, my right brain told me. Finally, after so very many disappointments today, an indulgence was mine for the taking.

The debate was very short.

Indulgence won with a capital *I*.

I didn't want to make Max guess, so I stripped off the little dress. I stood there in my panties, making myself perfectly clear.

I was in his arms in a flash, his embrace warm and engulfing. My breasts pressed against his bare chest, sending my arousal to new heights.

Then he lifted me like I weighed nothing. He started walking.

"Bedroom," he said.

My right brain cheered. It was probably the sexiest thing that had ever happened to me.

He carried me through a door to a second big room. Light filtered through an opaque blind, and I could make out a king-size bed, a padded headboard and a huge mound of pillows.

We collapsed together onto the soft bed, Max on top, propping himself with his elbows.

The quilt was smooth silk against my body. It was cool. A fan stirred the air overhead.

His hands clasped mine, and he moved in slow motion to kiss my lips.

I simultaneously moaned and sighed, melting against his mouth, then his thighs, then his chest as we pressed closer and tighter together.

His weight felt good. It felt sexy. It pushed me deep into the soft mattress.

His kisses were long and thorough, expertly sending messages to my breasts and inner thighs, making them tighten and buzz with desire.

His lips were magic. His hands did nothing but caress my palms, yet I was writhing and stretching and lifting my hips.

My panties were thin. So were his boxers. My thighs spread apart, and our touch through the whisper of fabric was a prelude to lovemaking.

I wanted him. I wanted him very badly.

I slipped my hands from his, wrapped my arms around him. He was steady and strong, like an anchor in a growing storm of desire.

He slipped off my panties and stripped off his boxers.

He produced a condom, then drew back to gaze into my eyes.

His were midnight blue, deep and dark in the weak light. Lashes framed their richness, their sensitivity, their intense passion.

"You okay?" he asked.

"I'm fantastic," I said.

He smiled then as he tore open the package. "You are all of that."

In seconds, his hips flexed and we were locked together.

"Still good?" he rasped.

"Oh, yeah."

His kisses began all over again.

His hands roamed my body, and mine roamed his.

He found all the points, and the spots—all the zones.

I indulged myself, tracing his iron biceps, bulging shoulders and the contours of his back. His hands were strong and broad, blunt and certain.

His rhythm was steady, teasing and building. I shifted my hips, tipping upward.

He rolled us together, slightly to one side, bringing a pillow beneath me before rocking back.

Pleasure rushed through me, leaving heat in its wake. Then again, and again.

"Oh, my." I gasped.

"Oh, yes," he said.

He wrapped me tight in his arms.

I clung to his shoulders, my fingertips gripping onto him tighter and tighter, hanging on as the world broke free.

I fell from the planet, throbbing, and I felt him follow.

The air was hot, perfumed and heavy. The sound of the fan whooshed loud above us. I could feel his deep breathing, the rise and fall of his chest, his heart beating hard, his sweat mingling with mine, and finally, the sweet weight of his limbs holding me fast.

Max spoke first. "That was…"

The fan circled a few more times.

"It was," I said.

He smoothed back my hair and lifted his head to meet my gaze.

"Layla," he whispered.

Then he tenderly kissed my mouth.

"Max," I said in return. I couldn't help but smile.

This was hands down the most amazing sex I'd ever had. I didn't know his secret, but I loved benefitting from it.

I was so satisfied.

I mean, sort of satisfied.

I mean, I was done…but I wasn't finished—not with Max, not with sex. It was a revelation. In this moment, I felt like I might never get enough of him.

He kissed me again, and I kissed him right back.

He kissed deeper and longer, and my arms went around him.

His hand covered my breast, and a quiver rolled through me.

His caress sharpened, and his kisses turned deliberate.

My energy roared to life, and arousal took serious root. Wherever he was going with this, I sure planned to follow.

In Max's bathroom, I was getting a sense of the opulence of the suite. The soaker tub was big enough for three. The multi-nozzle shower could host a party. And there were enough luxury bath products and plush towels to keep me happy…well, forever really.

I'd taken a quick shower and wrapped myself in one of the soft, white robes hanging in the bathroom closet. I hadn't yet gathered up my own clothes from the living room.

I wasn't so much looking forward to that part of the evening. Then again, I wasn't dreading it the way I ought to be dreading it, either.

I pulled down my hair, dried off the shower dampness with another of the towels. Then I used a little comb wrapped in a cellophane wrapper to tame the tangles. There was some nice-smelling lotion on the big marble counter, so I used a bit on my face and hands.

My mind began wandering to Max and how he could afford a hotel suite like this. Clearly he had means. He seemed intelligent, and he was definitely classy. How could it be that a great-looking guy like him was still single?

My brain paused for a minute, as single women's brains do. Was he married? He hadn't worn a ring—not that that meant anything. Lots of married guys didn't wear their rings when they traveled. I would imagine that went doubly for Vegas.

Then again, he might not be married.

I gazed at myself in the mirror and my brain insisted on going over the what-ifs. What if he wasn't married? What if he was everything he seemed? What if we fell madly in love, he wooed me around the world from London to Paris to Rome…?

Then I chuckled at myself in the mirror.

I was ridiculous.

This was a one-night stand. It might have been the greatest one-night stand in the history of one-night stands. But it was over. I was going to find Brooklyn and convince her to come back to San Francisco—or at this point maybe straight to Seattle. But I was going to find her and force her to come to her senses.

I was walking away from Max, and that was that.

I had to admit, I was glad we'd gone twice. It seemed more worthwhile that way.

I laughed at my reflection one more time before I left the dream bathroom.

Max was in the living room dressed in an identical robe. His hair was damp, and I could only conclude there was another bathroom somewhere in the rambling hotel suite.

I noticed my dress was neatly folded on an armchair. Since I hadn't seen my panties on the bedroom floor, I was guessing they were with the dress.

I gave a happy sigh inside. Guys like this sure *didn't* come along every day.

I headed for the dress. "I have to get going."

My guess was he wouldn't be disappointed to hear I was clearing out.

"You sure?" he asked.

My back was to him, but I strained to read his tone. Was that disappointment or relief I was hearing?

I shimmied into the panties. "I still have to find her."

My back to him, I dropped the robe and pulled the dress over my head.

There was a knock on the door.

It startled me, and I was weirdly embarrassed at being in Max's hotel room. I reminded myself that he might be married.

"Are you—"

"Can you hang on for just a second?" he asked.

"You want me to go in the bedroom?"

He gave me an odd look. "Not unless you want to."

My *married* odds moved from 50/50 to 25/75 in a good way.

I stayed put.

Max opened the door, and a waiter wheeled in a cart. I could see a champagne bottle and two glasses, and a big silver plate cover.

"Shall I set it up for you, Mr. Kendrick?"

"No thank you," Max said, handing something to the man.

I presumed it was a tip.

Max closed the door behind the waiter. "I thought you might be hungry."

"You didn't have to do that," I said, thinking his considerate gestures were getting a little out of hand.

"Come and look," he said with a self-satisfied smile.

I moved.

He lifted the plate cover.

The aroma hit me first. Chocolate soufflé.

"Are you serious?" I asked, even though I was staring right at it.

"I was sorry you had to miss it."

"You *replaced* our dessert?" After I'd so unceremoniously rushed away?

A teasing glint came into his eyes. "I hope you worked up an appetite."

For the first time, I felt self-conscious about our vigorous lovemaking. I wrapped my arms around myself.

His eyes dimmed a shade. "I'm sorry, Layla."

"No, no." I shook my head. "This was very thoughtful."

"I didn't mean to embarrass you."

"I'm not embarrassed."

"You look embarrassed."

"Well, now that we're making such a big deal of it. I guess I am. I'm standing here in the hotel room of a man I only just met who may or may not be married."

He drew back. "Whoa? *What?* I'm not married. What makes you think I'm married?"

I wasn't exactly sure how to phrase it—since now that he'd denied it, my suspicions seemed less rational.

"You didn't say you weren't," I said.

"I told you I wasn't a cheater."

I remembered our earlier conversation. "That was about a girlfriend."

"Seriously? A wife trumps a girlfriend, don't you think?"

I didn't have an answer for that. I mean, there was an obvious answer for that, so I didn't bother to say it out loud.

"Why didn't you just ask?"

He had me there. "I, uh, didn't think of it 'til later."

He looked thoughtful. "I guess I didn't, either. You're not married, are you?"

For a split second, I was offended. Then I realized it was a ridiculous reaction. He couldn't know it about me any more than I could have known it about him.

My embarrassment disappeared, replaced by self-deprecating humor. "Why didn't you just ask?"

"I was too intent on making love with you."

"I'm not married," I said.

He heaved an exaggerated sigh of relief. "Now that we have that out of the way." He then glanced to the soufflé. "Are you going to let this get cold?"

"No." I wasn't giving up the decadent dessert a second time.

Max took the soufflé and the bottle of champagne, and I brought along the glasses and plates. We settled corner-wise from each other on the padded chairs of a big dining room table.

"So are you some überwealthy—" I glanced around the place "—like prince or something?"

He laughed as he popped the champagne cork.

"This is just business," he said.

"What does that mean?"

Max nodded. "It means the corporation gets a really big discount. So don't be too impressed."

"What kind of business."

He filled my glass with the bubbling champagne. "Do we really have to talk business?"

I was curious, but I wasn't going to be annoying about it. "I suppose not."

"I want to pretend I'm on vacation."

"I wish I was on vacation."

He raised his glass.

I did as well.

"To vacations."

"I will definitely drink to that."

Once this was all over, and James and Brooklyn were safely married, I was seriously considering going on a vacation. I figured I was going to deserve it.

The champagne was crisp, smooth and ridiculously delicious. And I ate every bite of my soufflé while Max talked about his kayak trip to Angel Island.

So he did row...well, paddle, I guess. But he stayed in shape. He definitely stayed in shape.

Too soon the champagne bottle was empty.

"I have to go," I said again.

Brooklyn was still out there.

He took my hand lightly in his. "Stay here. With me."

I shook my head. As comfortable as I felt with him, we had only just met and spending the night in his hotel room seemed way too intimate, even if a part of me desperately wanted to sleep in his arms.

"Why?"

"You and I just met."

He thought for a moment before nodding. "Too soon?"

"Too soon."

I couldn't stop myself from liking the implication that there might be a *later*, an *again*, possibly a *future*. It didn't matter that I was getting way ahead of myself again. Max was one great guy, and if only for this moment, it felt like this could be the start of something.

He was quiet, thinking again. Maybe he'd try to change

my mind. Maybe my mind could be changed. Maybe I was being too hasty in turning down his offer.

"What if you don't find her?" he asked.

"I'll have to…eventually."

"You're planning to wander the lobby all night long?"

I had to admit, I hadn't thought through past midnight or so. All of my plans ended with me finding Brooklyn. There were night flights back to San Francisco. We'd take one.

"Let me get you a room," Max said.

I didn't understand what he meant.

"At the corporate discount," he said, moving to pick up a hotel phone.

"You can't—"

"Sure I can. If you find her, no harm, no foul. If you don't, there'll be a room waiting when you decide you have to sleep."

I opened my mouth to protest again. But then I stopped myself. He was right, and I was going to be logical about it. If I didn't find Brooklyn tonight, my best bet was to try again tomorrow. I'd rather sleep in a discounted room than in a lobby armchair.

Unless I stayed with Max… Which I couldn't. I wouldn't. I had to trust my left brain on that.

"This is Max Kendrick," he said into the phone. "Can you book a tentative reservation under the name of Layla Gillen?" He paused. "One night. Is there anything available on thirty-five?"

He covered the mouthpiece and whispered, "Might as well have a view of the Strip."

I didn't need a view of the Strip. I'd rather take a bargain room overlooking the mechanical wing. Even at a corporate discount, this was going to hurt.

"Perfect," he said into the phone. "Thanks." He hung

up and returned to his chair. "The key will be waiting at the front desk if you need it."

"What's the damage?" I asked, bracing myself. Maybe I would sleep in the lobby.

"Seventy-six thirty-two."

The figure wasn't computing inside my head. Surely to goodness, Max wouldn't have booked me a seven-thousand-dollar hotel room. "How much did you say?" My voice squeaked embarrassingly.

"Seventy-six dollars and thirty-two cents."

Wait, what? "That doesn't even make sense."

"I told you we had a good discount. You're basically just paying the tax."

Something didn't seem right to me. "They're giving me a free room."

"No, they're giving a good corporate client a free room. It's empty. Nobody's going to sleep in it if you don't."

"Let me point out the flaws in that logic," I said.

"Please don't."

"You can't operate at a loss and make it up in volume."

He smiled and reached out to cradle my cheek. "I'm pretty sure the Canterbury Sands isn't operating at a loss."

"They will be if they keep doing things like this." I leaned my face into his palm.

I wanted to stay. I really, desperately wanted to stay.

"You want help finding your friend?" Max asked.

"I'll be fine."

I told myself to stand up, but my legs didn't move. Then I ordered myself to stand up. Unfortunately, myself wasn't cooperating very well tonight.

"I have to go now," I said to myself as much as to Max.

"Okay," he said.

"Thank you for…" I wasn't exactly sure how to phrase it.

"Dessert?" he asked with a lift of one eyebrow.

"Dessert," I agreed with a smile. "It was a really lovely dessert."

I managed to force myself to stand.

He stood with me. "If it gets late, pick up the key." Then he gave me a tender kiss on the lips. The tingle told me mine were bruised—in a good way, a very good way.

I wanted to melt against him. But I knew that would be the end of my Brooklyn search. I owed it to my brother and to Brooklyn to stay strong.

"Goodbye, Max Kendrick. It was nice to meet you."

"It was nice to meet you, Layla Gillen."

Four

I set my alarm, and it's a good thing I did, because I was sound asleep when "Viva la Vida" came up on my phone.

My room was nowhere near the size of Max's. But it was beautiful and comfortable, and the view was off the charts. I was seriously thinking of applying for a job with whatever corporation he worked for. The vacation perks alone would be worth it.

I wondered again what he did for a living—also if there was a chance they needed a mathematician.

I wished I could luxuriate in the shower or maybe take a long bath in the jet tub. But I wasn't here for pleasure. I had to get back on Brooklyn's trail. So I pushed myself through a quick morning routine and headed for the lobby again.

In the Sweet Garden Restaurant, I found her. There was no mistake this time. I was looking at her head-on. And she was in the middle of the room with no quick exit.

I had her.

Intent on Brooklyn, I was almost to the table before I looked at her companion.

I stopped, froze really. Everything inside me turned ice-cold, and a roar came up inside my brain.

"You!" I called out, almost shouting.

The tables nearby went quiet, and I thought to move closer.

"You!" I rasped this time in a whisper.

Max stared at me in abject shock, all but dropping his fork into his scrambled eggs.

"Layla," Brooklyn said, guilt and astonishment ringing clear in her tone. "What are you doing here?"

I turned my head, frustrated with her but purely incensed with Max. "I'm here for you. I came to talk to you. I came to bring you to your senses. Why wouldn't you answer your phone?"

I struggled to make sense of the situation.

Had Max known who I was all along? Was he psychologically deranged?

"I didn't know what to tell you," Brooklyn said.

I turned back to Max. "What is this? Are you sick? Are you a pervert?"

He looked baffled by the question.

I kept talking. "Why would you do such a horrible, horrible thing?"

"Layla," Brooklyn cried out. "It's not his fault."

My focus remained glued on Max. "How is it not his fault? *How* is it not your fault?"

He'd slept with me. He was wooing Brooklyn by day and sleeping with her best friend by night?

"It's just happened," Brooklyn said. "We didn't plan it."

Max sat there silently.

Max, who'd kissed me so passionately, who'd held me tenderly in his arms, who'd taken me to heights of pleasure and then ordered chocolate soufflé.

"Tell her what you did," I said to Max. *"Tell her!"*

"Layla?" Now Brooklyn sounded worried.

"She doesn't know, does she?" I said to Max. "Do you feel the least bit guilty? Are you twisted?"

"Layla!" Brooklyn came to her feet. "I know this has to be hard for you."

Max stood, as well.

"He's a lying scumbag," I said to Brooklyn. "Let's go. Let's go right now and forget any of this ever happened."

I was having second thoughts about telling Brooklyn the whole truth about Max. Maybe she didn't need to know. Maybe this was a secret I should take to my grave.

The important thing here was that she came back to James. She could choose James over Max without ever knowing the depths of Max's depravity.

"You must be Layla," Max said to me.

I felt like my head might explode. "That's how you're going to play it?"

"Play what?"

I glared at him.

He stared back. His acting was superb.

"Layla?" A voice behind me joined the conversation.

It was weird.

It was stereo.

I turned to see Max standing behind me. The loud noise came up in my ears again, and my knees went wobbly.

"Layla?" Brooklyn asked from what seemed like a long distance away.

"Whoa." Max reached for my arm and took hold of me.

"Who?" I managed to ask.

I gaped at the Max behind me.

"I see you've met my brother, Colton," Max said.

"Are you kidding me?" Colton said to Max.

"Me kidding you?" Max asked. "What on earth's going on?"

"You met Brooklyn," Colton said to Max.

"*This* is the guy?" I said to Brooklyn.

"This is Colton Kendrick," Brooklyn said.

Her face was flushed. Well, she should be embarrassed.

"Brooklyn is engaged," I told Colton flatly.

"I'm aware of that," Colton said.

"So, what—"

"What are you doing?" Max's question rolled right over mine.

"It's complicated," Colton said to Max.

"It's simple," I said, my gaze taking in both Colton and Brooklyn. "Brooklyn is marrying my brother, James, in thirteen days at St. Fidelis's Cathedral. It's been planned for over a year, and there are five hundred guests coming."

Colton looked to Brooklyn and raised his brow. "Five hundred?"

"That's relevant?" she asked him.

"It's unsettling."

"Get over it—"

"Hey," I interrupted. "Can we take a reality check here?"

"Your brother?" Max asked me.

"They've been in love for years," I said.

"That *is* complicated," Max said.

"Not you, too."

Max gestured to Brooklyn and Colton. "It looks complicated to me."

"It's fleeting," I said, knowing it had to be true. "It's a phase, nothing more."

"Why don't we ask them about that?"

It occurred to me that I should be having this conversation with Brooklyn. It had nothing to do with Max. Max and I were done.

All night long and through the morning I'd hoped I would see him one more time. Now I never wanted to see him again. My memories of last night would always be tainted by these horrible circumstances.

"Can we go somewhere and talk?" I asked Brooklyn. The best thing I could do in this moment was to get her out of Colton's clutches.

She looked to Colton before answering.

That reaction was not encouraging.

"Go," he said gently. "You can't hide anymore."

The reluctance on Brooklyn's face hit me square in the stomach.

She was my best friend. We shared everything. I couldn't remember a single time, a single event, a single moment when she hadn't wanted to pour out her heart to me, and me to her. This man was coming between more than James and Brooklyn. He was coming between me and my best friend.

He had to be stopped.

Brooklyn headed down the hallway that I'd learned led to the hotel garden.

We didn't talk as we wound our way through the morning crowds.

She took a different route, but we ended up at the Triple Palm Café. It was quiet this morning, and we easily found a table by the rail overlooking the gardens.

As soon as the waitress finished pouring coffee and orange juice, I launched into the speech I'd been mentally rehearsing for hours.

"What is going on?" I demanded, but I didn't stop for an answer or even a breath. "You sneak out of the hotel room, leave me this stupid note, ignore your phone and shack up with some guy—"

"He's not just some guy, and we didn't shack up."

"Do you know him? Had you met him before Friday night?"

I could tell by Brooklyn's expression that the answer was no.

"Then he's just some guy," I said. "You've known James for years. You've *loved* James for years."

"I didn't plan this." Brooklyn's voice cracked ever so slightly, evoking an unwanted swell of sympathy inside me.

I didn't want to be sympathetic. I wasn't anywhere near ready to consider her side of the story. I was in full-on defense mode of my brother.

"I didn't want this," she said.

I kept my voice hard. "Then why did you do it?"

She scanned the garden as if she was framing her answer.

"Why?" I repeated.

"It's Colton," she said. "He's… We're… It's…"

"Do you have a brain tumor?" I asked. For the first time it occurred to me that this situation might not be Brooklyn's fault.

She rolled her eyes and lifted her coffee cup to take a sip. "I do not have a brain tumor."

"I've heard that people's personalities can totally change when they have a brain tumor. Do you need a CAT scan?"

"No."

"We can get you a CAT scan. I bet we can get one right here in Vegas, today. If there's something wrong with your brain—"

"There's nothing wrong with my brain. My brain is perfectly fine, thank you very much."

"How would you know?"

Now that I'd come up with the theory, I realized it had merit. This was a complete and sudden departure from the woman I'd known my whole life. Something like this didn't happen, all of a sudden, out of the blue, with no warning whatsoever, if there was nothing physically wrong with a person's brain.

"Maybe it was a stroke," I said.

"Will you stop?"

"A ministroke. You remember my Aunt Sandy had one that time. You'd never have known it happened if she didn't develop the sudden poker addiction. She had all of her friends playing five-card stud for quarters. Before we figured it out, she won two hundred bucks and made Rachel Simms cry."

"A stroke?" Brooklyn asked. "Seriously?"

"It could happen."

"I'm twenty-six years old."

"I know that."

"Then you know I didn't have a stroke."

"Then *what on earth is wrong with you*?"

Brooklyn took another sip of her coffee.

This time I joined her. It was hard to carry on a decent argument in the morning without a shot of caffeine.

The waitress reappeared before Brooklyn could answer.

"Can I get you something from the menu?" she asked.

"An oatmeal muffin for me," Brooklyn said.

"A waffle," I said. "Make it with strawberries, whipped cream and chocolate topping." I figured it was the least I deserved given the stress of the circumstances.

Brooklyn looked surprised.

"It's not like I have to fit into my bridesmaid dress." I hoped the pithy comment shook her back to reality.

"I guess," she said, sounding hesitant.

I took in the nuances of her expression. "So you haven't completely made up your mind."

"I…"

I reached out and touched her hand. "Brooklyn, hon, shut this down before it's too late."

Remorse crossed her face. "Do Sophie and Nat know?"

I was reminded that I should text Sophie and Nat. "I didn't show them the note. Nobody but me knows about this."

Brooklyn gave a small, sad smile. "Thanks."

I pulled out my phone to text Sophie.

"What are you doing?" Brooklyn looked worried.

"I'm telling them I found you. I'll say you needed a night alone. I'll tell them we're coming back today."

"No."

I met her gaze, telling myself to be calm and patient. Brooklyn was rattled and confused, and I had to bring her back down to earth. "We have to go back," I said.

"I can't go back."

"Well, you can't stay here." I looked around at the meticulous, sculpted trees, the perfect gardens, the lights, the fountains. "This is a fantasy, Brooklyn. *He's* a fantasy."

"He's not."

"You don't even know him."

"Maybe not, not completely yet, but he's… There's something about him, Layla, something big, something huge, something I've never felt before, not even with—"

"James. Your fiancé. The man you love."

Her eyes took on a sheen of tears. "I do love James."

Now we were getting somewhere. I felt myself relax for the first time in two days.

"Thing is—" she traced the condensation on her orange-juice glass "—I'm not *in* love with James."

"That doesn't even make sense." My momentary optimism shifted. It turned to a block of cement in my stomach. "You're not making sense, Brooklyn."

"I wanted to be your sister."

This time I squeezed her hand. "You *are* my sister."

"I love your family."

"We love you. We all love you. It's going to be great. The future is going to be wonderful."

All she had to do was get up from this table, get into a cab with me and head for the airport. There were flights back to San Francisco all day long. We'd take one and forget this ever happened.

My mind flashed to Max.

Okay, so maybe I wouldn't forget every little thing about this ever happened. Even though I wanted to, my night with Max wasn't something I'd ever forget.

"You're not listening," Brooklyn said.

"That's because you don't know what you're saying."

She shook her head. "No. It's because you can't let go of the fantasy we spun, that I spun, that I let everyone believe in for so long. I am sorry, you know."

"Stop." I couldn't hear this.

Our breakfasts arrived, and we both took a breath.

The waffle looked fantastic, but I wasn't sure I could eat anything right now.

"I convinced myself I was in love with James."

"No." I'd seen them together. I'd watched them for years. It wasn't an act. "You've convinced yourself you're not."

"I just found out there's a world of difference."

"You've known that man—"

"Colton."

"Fine. Colton." His name felt like acid on my tongue. "You've known *Colton* for two days—*two days*."

"It's not like I'm going to up and marry him at an Elvis chapel."

"This isn't funny."

"It's a little bit funny."

"Brooklyn!" I didn't know what was wrong with her, but it was something profound.

"If we don't laugh, we're going to have to cry."

"You're destroying your life, and James's life, and my life." It made perfect sense that we should cry.

She split her muffin in two. "I'm changing our lives."

"Not for the better."

"You don't know that."

I picked up my fork and stared at the whipped cream melting over my waffle. The warm chocolate syrup was pooling on the plate. I suddenly felt tired. "Let's go home, Brooklyn."

"Stay," she said, her gaze turning warm, open and cajoling. She finally looked like regular Brooklyn again—the way she looked when she wanted something—free milkshakes for example.

"Make an excuse to Sophie and Nat, and stay here with me a couple of days."

"You want me to watch you date Colton?"

"I want you to meet him. You've met Max." Suddenly, her expression turned calculating.

I felt like I'd been slid under a microscope. I didn't like it.

"You've met Max," she repeated. It was clear the wheels were turning inside her head. "How did that happen? When did that happen? What happened?"

"We had dinner," I said. "And he helped me get a discount hotel room."

I was going to tell her the whole story. I wouldn't keep it from her forever. I just couldn't tell her right now, not right this minute. She'd latch onto it, and the discussion of my sex life would distract from the central problem—which was that she had gotten confused.

Then the wheels took a turn inside my head. "Wait. *You'd* already met Max?"

I couldn't help but wonder what Colton had told Max about Brooklyn. Was it possible Max had known or suspected I was Brooklyn's friend? Could he have been keeping me away from Brooklyn to help his brother?

That was a particularly mortifying thought. I'd hopped into his bed when maybe all he was doing was keeping me occupied for a few hours. We might just as well have done karaoke.

"I only met Max in passing," Brooklyn said. "Just for a minute when we first got here."

"Does Max know about James?"

"I don't see how. I've been with Colton the whole time, and Max only knew I was Colton's date. I got the impression Colton and Max have a lot of dates."

Well, there was another unsettling revelation. There was a reason Max was so suave and sophisticated during a one-night stand. He was good at it because he'd had practice.

My brain kept trailing its way to Max. But I knew I had to stay focused.

"So Colton knows about James." I was deciding how drastically to loathe Colton Kendrick.

Before she answered, Brooklyn cracked a soft, intimate smile.

I didn't like the looks of that, not at all.

"Colton knows all about James," she said.

I instantly made my decision. I completely loathed Colton.

Brooklyn wouldn't leave Vegas, and I wasn't going back without her.

It was all Colton's fault that I was maxing out my credit

card at the Canterbury Sands Hotel. Sure, Max had bought me dinner last night and Brooklyn had signed breakfast to her room—not that I'd even tasted my waffle. But my free ride was now over.

Brooklyn had gone to meet Colton, and I was in the check-in line wondering if I dared ask about getting a corporate rate. If I'd known the name of the company where Max worked, I might have given it a try. But without that piece of information, I didn't think there was any way I'd pull off the ruse.

I wondered if Max and Colton might work for the same company. That would explain why they'd both been at the Archway at the same time, and why they were here in Vegas at the same time. Brothers could go on vacation together, of course. But Max had said they were on business. So them being in the same business made the most sense to me.

It seemed weird, being a twin, growing up together and then working together. That was a lot of togetherness. Don't get me wrong, I love my family. But I can't see spending every weekday with any of them.

There were three people left in front of me when Max appeared.

"How did it go?" he asked.

"Did you know?" I asked outright. Brooklyn might not have told Max the whole story, but that didn't mean Colton hadn't found a way to share it with his twin brother.

"Know what?" Max asked.

I judged the space between us and the couple in front, then lowered my voice. "That Brooklyn was engaged to my brother."

"How would I know that?"

"From Colton. *Your* brother."

"I didn't. And, anyway, you never told me Brooklyn's name. How would I have put the two things together?"

He made a fair point.

I wasn't one hundred percent convinced, but I'd say I was ninety-five.

"I'm taking her back," I told him. "Colton can't have her."

Max obviously fought a smirk. "Don't you think that's up to Brooklyn?"

"She's not thinking straight. She'll come around."

"So you're staying for a while."

It wasn't a question, since there was no other reason for me to be in the check-in line.

"I'm not staying long. She'll come to her senses. Hopefully today."

I'd texted Sophie and Nat and told them they should head back to Seattle without us. I'd also sent a message to James telling him Brooklyn and I were taking an extra day to chill out before the wedding.

It was mostly true. We were taking an extra day on vacation. And I told myself *chilling* was a matter of degree. We were chilling a little bit.

My turn came and Max walked up to the counter with me.

"You can check Ms. Gillen in under an *H* rate," he said to the female clerk.

"Of course, Mr. Kendrick." She gave him a warm smile.

"Do you know *everybody*?" I asked him.

The woman glanced my way with a puzzled expression.

"I'm a friendly guy," Max said to me.

"Any preference on the room?" the woman asked, her gaze going from Max to me and back again.

"Did you like your room last night?" Max asked me.

"The view was off-the-charts." I'd easily admit that for seventy-six dollars a night, I'd take that room all week long.

"She was on the thirty-fifth floor," Max said to the clerk.

"I really appreciate this," I said to Max. And I did. Whatever else was going on here, he was saving me a fortune.

"No problem."

"Do you have a preference for a north or south view?" the woman asked me this time.

"Either is fine." Even if I did know the difference, I wasn't going to act like a princess.

"Thirty-five-oh-seven or fourteen?" Max asked.

The woman hit a couple of keys. "Thirty-five-oh-seven is available."

"Make it for three nights," Max said.

"I'm not going to be—"

"You can always cancel."

"It's not going to take anywhere near that long."

"Better to have a backup plan," he said.

"Oh, I have a backup plan all right."

The clerk handed me a key card.

"Do tell," Max said as we walked away.

I knew my way to the elevators. "Give my plan to an agent of the enemy? I don't think so."

"I'm not the enemy."

"Colton is the enemy."

"Colton is a very principled guy."

"He's seducing an engaged woman. How is that a principled guy?"

We came to the elevator bank and Max pressed the button. "Is that how you see it?"

It occurred to me that there was little point in going up to the room. It wasn't like I had anything to unpack. I was going to have to pick up a few things today, under-wear for one.

I'd washed my panties in the sink last night and dried them with the hair dryer. But it would be a whole lot eas-ier if I had an extra pair.

The hotel had provided the basics, like a toothbrush and toothpaste. It would also be nice to change my clothes. My best vacation clothes were going home to Seattle with Sophie and Nat.

The hotel shops were superexpensive, but I didn't want to leave Brooklyn alone with Colton any longer than ab-solutely necessary. She'd promised to answer her phone when I called from now on. And I planned to call her very soon and meet up.

I stepped into the elevator and Max followed. We were the only two in the car.

"I can take it from here," I said.

The thought of him in my room gave me a little thrill. I thought if we were alone again, he might kiss me. Or I might kiss him. I didn't want to want him all over again, but there wasn't a whole lot I could do about my attraction.

"Room service can deliver anything from the hotel shops," Max said. "If you need clothes or cosmetics."

"You think I need makeup?" I asked.

I usually wore a little bit, but it was another thing that stayed back in San Francisco when I left in a hurry.

"I didn't say that."

"You don't think I'm pretty enough?"

I didn't want to be fishing for a compliment, but it turned out I wanted one. I found myself questioning his motivations again. It wasn't like I'd looked my best, ei-ther yesterday or today. And I had a feeling Max looked his best 24/7. At least he looked that way to me. I'd truly never met a more attractive man.

"You have a mirror," he said.

It wasn't exactly the flattering remark I'd been hoping for. Then again, it ought to be a lesson to me.

The elevator accelerated smoothly upward.

"What's your deal?" I asked.

"My deal?"

"Is this a favor for your brother?"

"Is what a favor for my brother?"

"Hanging out with me, keeping me busy, keeping the field clear with Brooklyn."

"No."

"I don't believe you."

It made perfect sense. Colton wanted Brooklyn, and he knew I wanted to take her away. I didn't yet have a bead on Colton's motives. I didn't buy for a second that he was as delusional as Brooklyn over their soul-mate-ness. So probably he just thought she was gorgeous and fun and friendly and smart.

She was all of those things. It was why James loved her.

"You seem extraordinarily devoted to your brother," Max said.

"I'm completely ordinarily devoted to my brother and to all the other members of my family."

"Well, I'm not."

"You don't even know my family." It came as a bit of a surprise to me that I'd crack a joke.

"Ha, ha. I mean Colton's on his own when it comes to his relationships. He doesn't need me as a wingman."

"Sure." Skepticism colored my tone.

Friends were always wingmen. Brothers were even better wingmen. I could only imagine twin brothers were the top of the heap. How could a person not be loyally devoted to their twin brother?

"You're a skeptical woman, Layla Gillen."

"I think you mean astute."

We arrived at the thirty-fifth floor and exited the elevator. I held the card to the lock and heard the tumblers click.

"I don't know why I even came up here," I said.

I had nothing to drop off or pick up. Okay. I should call Brooklyn and get her to meet me somewhere. Hopefully, she'd had a chance to think about all the things I'd said.

Liking my plan, I entered the hotel room and was immediately struck by the view.

The room was slightly bigger than last night's. It was on a corner with two walls of glass and a small sitting area overlooking feature hotels, fountains and the giant Ferris wheel just off the Strip.

I didn't want to love it, but I did.

I found myself drawn to the glass wall. "This one costs more, doesn't it?"

"A little," Max said.

The door banged shut behind him.

"What are we talking, eighty dollars, eighty-two fifty?"

"Something like that."

"Do you live like this all the time?"

I loved my job, I really did. Teaching was rewarding, and I loved the kids, and I dearly loved living close to my family. But there was something exotic and exciting about fine hotel rooms in iconic cities, where you didn't have to cook, run errands or make a bed.

They'd deliver new clothes if I asked. Who wouldn't love that? At least for a while. I'd like to fantasize about living that way for at least a little while.

"It can get old," Max said, and I realized he'd moved closer.

"Go ahead, burst my bubble."

He animated his voice. "But the perks can be great."

"No dishes."

"Somebody washes your sheets and cleans your shower."

"It could make a person feel lazy."

"I suppose." He brushed his hand lightly across my shoulder.

A sigh of contentment rolled all the way through me. His touch had been magic last night, and I could feel the arousal start all over again. It was like my hormones remembered. They remembered Max and they craved him now.

"Layla." His voice was deep.

I felt it in my chest and in the pit of my abdomen.

I wanted so badly to lean back into him, to feel his arms around me, his kiss on my neck, his hands...well, everywhere.

Shut up, right brain.

I squeezed my hands hard against the urge, and I felt the rectangle of my phone against my palm.

I summoned my strength. "I have to call Brooklyn."

Max's sigh was audible.

"She needs me," I said.

There was an edge of impatience to his tone. "If you say so."

"This isn't a game."

"Nobody said it was a game."

I turned to face him. It was a risk. My desire for him was acute and insistent. But I needed him to understand. "I'm not going to do this," I said.

"Do what?"

"Don't play dumb. I'm not going to muddle things up by kissing you...or worse."

"I wouldn't call it worse. I'd call it better." He grinned.

"Worse. It would be worse. I'm disgusted by your brother."

Something flinched in Max's expression.

I found it admirable that he'd want to defend Colton. It was admirable, but it didn't change my mind in the least.

Brooklyn was mine and she was James's. Colton would just have to accept that. And that I was going to win her back.

"We're adversaries in this." I figured we might as well have it out on the table.

"It's none of our business."

I coughed out a laugh at that. "It's entirely my business. And he's your brother. So keep your distance." I took a step back to emphasize my point.

"And what if I can't?"

I didn't believe that for a second. "Summon your strength."

"For you, I will try."

I rolled my eyes. "For me. Right. I'm calling Brooklyn now." I touched her contact name and put the phone to my ear.

"Let me know how it goes," he said.

I was about to point out that we wouldn't be having any future conversations during which I would tell him anything at all. But true to her word, Brooklyn answered her phone on the first ring.

Max gave me a mock salute and headed for the door.

"Layla?" Brooklyn asked into the silence. "Are you there?"

Five

"I'm here," I said to Brooklyn.

"Where's here?"

"My hotel room. I have a room now."

"That's good." She went silent for a moment. "Colton says he can get you a rate."

"Max already did."

"Max is there?" Brooklyn sounded intrigued.

The door clicked shut behind him.

"No, he's not. I met him in the lobby."

I really didn't like this new me who told Brooklyn half truths. Normally, I'd dish the dirt, however bad it was.

If this was a normal time, I'd be telling Brooklyn all about my confusing feelings for Max, how he turned me on and made me laugh, and how I had to fight those feelings for James's benefit. But these weren't normal times, and I sure couldn't tell those things to Brooklyn.

"Well, good on the rate," she said. "I saw the rack rates posted on the back of the door. That'll cut into the 401K."

"What company do they work for?" I asked.

"What? Who?"

"Max and… Never mind. Where are you?"

"In the car."

My heart sank a little. "You're leaving?"

"No, we're coming back. We did some shopping."

"For what?"

Brooklyn had brought her suitcase with her from San Francisco. Surely she didn't need any new clothes. I suspected Colton was trying to woo her with expensive gifts, perfume and jewelry.

For some reason I pictured a fancy engagement ring. Well, she already had one of those.

Then I thought back to this morning and wondered if she'd been wearing it. I wasn't sure. I hadn't thought to check.

"For you," she said.

I'd lost the train of our conversation. "Huh?"

"I bought you some clothes, something for the pool. Want to meet me there?"

"You bought me clothes."

"Yes."

"You and Colton bought me clothes."

"What is wrong with you? I'm not explaining Fermat's Last Theorem."

"You don't understand Fermat's Last Theorem."

"I know."

"*I*, on the other hand, do understand it. Because I have a master's degree in mathematics, and I had to study that kind of thing." I had no idea why I was going off on a tangent. Maybe I was unsettled by the idea of Colton doing such an ordinary thing with Brooklyn as buying a bathing suit. It was one thing to woo her with extravagance, but this was everyday life.

She and I were the same size. We bought each other clothes and borrowed each other's clothes all the time.

"It's a yellow-and-black two-piece, with this cute crocheted cover-up."

I did need a new swimsuit. Brooklyn knew that. She'd teased me about packing my old aqua-blue standby.

"We can get tall, frozen margaritas on the pool deck."

I was gazing out at the sunshine and blue skies. With all I'd been through the past couple of days, a deck chair and a margarita sounded pretty good.

"Will I have to mortgage the condo to buy one?" I asked.

"They're on Colton."

"Colton is *not* bribing me."

"What bribing? He's trying to liquor you up so you'll be happy."

"I'm not happy. I'm never going to be happy until you come to your senses."

"Fine. But in the meantime, let's mellow you out with tequila."

"Okay," I reluctantly said. There was really nothing for me to do alone in the hotel room.

If I was lucky, Brooklyn would come to the pool by herself. If I wasn't, I might be able to separate her from Colton by suggesting a swim. I was determined to get her away from him as much as possible.

"The Vista pool on the twenty-sixth floor. We'll be there in ten."

I ended the call and headed for the bathroom to put my hair up out of the way.

I found a hotel tote bag and a small bottle of suntan lotion.

I dropped my key card and the lotion into the tote bag, locked my purse in the little safe and took the elevator down to twenty-six.

Brooklyn and Colton were already there.

Colton looked so much like Max that I did a double take. But then he smiled, and I knew it wasn't Max.

Colton looked buttoned-down and professional, a little un-approachable. Max came across as open and warm, even when you didn't know him. I thought his irises might be a shade darker than Colton's, his lips a little fuller and his eyebrows slightly heavier.

Brooklyn waved a purple shopping bag. "I bought you some new sandals, too."

"Thanks," I said as I approached.

"Hello, Layla," Colton said.

Brooklyn handed me the bag.

"Hello, Colton." I wouldn't be friendly. But I wouldn't be nasty, either. "Thank you for this."

"No problem."

"Oh, I can see this is going to be fun," Brooklyn said. "Both of you, lighten up."

"I'm not feeling light," I said.

"I can be light," Colton said.

He didn't look light. He looked wary.

I couldn't really blame him for that. I was his girl-friend's fiancé's sister after all. I hoped he felt wary...and guilty. I hoped he felt both wary and guilty. He deserved to feel that way.

"You should put on your suit," Brooklyn said to me.

She looked around the pool deck, then pointed. "We'll go over there, under the striped blue umbrella, the one that's open."

"Okay," I said.

It did look like a great spot, in front of a couple of palm trees, beside a Plexiglas railing.

"I'll get the drinks," Colton said. "Lime margarita okay with you?" he asked me.

"Sure." I didn't like myself for accepting his hospital-ity while being so cold to him. "Charge it to my room."

"Don't be ridiculous," he said, moving on to Brooklyn. "Lime?" he asked her.

"Mango," she said.

He smiled.

His eyes grew warmer, softer, when he looked at Brooklyn.

I could see why she thought he was in love.

I turned and shook the image out of my head. Colton wasn't in love with Brooklyn. Colton barely knew Brooklyn. Whatever he was feeling was superficial and likely to disappear at any moment.

I was puzzled as to why Brooklyn was buying into his infatuation. Guys had been falling for her at first sight since we'd turned fourteen. She always brushed it off, laughed it off, took the free milkshake or martini and went on her way.

I wondered what was different this time as I let myself into the richly appointed changing room off the pool deck. The walls were a warm peach, with a matching marble floor. The decor was accented with polished cedar benches and cubical doors.

The countertops were decorated with baskets of the same high-end toiletries I'd found in my room. I hadn't needed to bring my own suntan lotion. There were five choices, all different strengths, here for the taking.

I changed into the suit and cover-up. It fit perfectly, and looked terrific. Brooklyn always did have great taste in clothes. I tucked my jeans, blouse and underwear into the tote bag, helped myself to a striped beach towel from the shelf by the door and headed back out to the pool deck.

I decided that if I could find a way to ignore Colton, this could be a perfectly pleasant afternoon.

The deck loungers looked cushy and comfy. The buzz of conversation on the deck was just right. There was music in the background, but it was low and flowing, keeping with the laid-back mood of the pool deck.

I saw a waiter carrying a tray of frosty, garnished margaritas. They looked good. In fact, they looked delicious.

As I walked, the waiter stayed ahead of me, then he set down the drinks on the table next to Brooklyn.

Colton had settled on the opposite side of her, so I took the lounger across the table. It had been set up with plush fitted toweling with a folded towel waiting for me at the foot. I realized, again, I hadn't needed to bring my own supplies.

"You look great," Brooklyn said as she handed one of the lime margaritas across to Colton.

"Thanks for this," I said. "I love it."

"I knew it was you the second I saw it."

"She did," Colton said.

I wished I didn't have to acknowledge him, but that would be unforgivably rude.

I settled for making the oblique point that I had known Brooklyn her whole life. "Brooklyn's always had great taste in clothes. Even when we were kids."

Colton's smile said he knew exactly what I was doing.

Well, that was annoying.

"I'm learning all kinds of great things about Brooklyn," he said.

"Are you two going to be snotty?" Brooklyn asked.

"I think so," I said.

Colton grinned.

"Well, get it out of your system, I guess." She stripped off her gauzy bikini cover-up, plopped her sunglasses over her eyes and settled back on the lounger.

I looked at Colton, and he looked back at me.

"She's in love with my brother," I said.

"I respect that."

His answer was preposterous.

"No, you don't."

"I respect that she gets to make up her own mind."

I didn't have a ready answer for that. I couldn't disagree with it. But Brooklyn wasn't currently in her right mind, so it didn't really count.

I took a drink of my margarita, stalling for time.

"You disagree?" he asked, clearly sensing his advantage in the conversation.

"I think you've only just met each other."

"True." He nodded. "But there's enough that we know we need to give it a shot."

"Damn the torpedoes?" I asked. "Just test it out and see where it leads, no matter what kind of destruction you leave in your wake?"

"Layla," Brooklyn said.

"It's okay," Colton said. "She's entitled to her opinion."

I summoned my best sarcastic tone. "Thank you so much."

To my annoyance, Colton grinned again. "Brooklyn told me you were feisty."

"I'm not feisty."

Brooklyn lifted her glasses and opened one eye to look at me. "Are you kidding me?"

"Well, of course, I'm *feisty*. But my feistiness is not the reason for my reaction to this preposterous situation. I'm also logical and reasonable. I'm a mathematician, and this is completely illogical."

"I don't think love follows a mathematical formula," Brooklyn said.

"It obeys the laws of statistics and probability. Everything does."

"There are outliers," Colton said. He reached for Brooklyn's hand.

"We're outliers," she said.

I wanted to yank them apart, but I couldn't reach from here. Coming to my feet and marching around Brooklyn's lounger to pull their hands apart seemed ridiculously dramatic, not to mention futile.

I needed a better plan than that.

I took another long drink of the margarita, sitting back and moving my attention to the water polo game at the far end of the pool. I knew full well that tequila didn't improve a person's decision-making capabilities. But the drink was delicious, and lowering my stress level would at least help me cope with the problem—even if I couldn't fix it right at this moment.

One of the teams scored, and a cheer came up.

Behind them, a movement caught my eye.

Max.

He was wearing black swim trunks and nothing else, strolling across the deck as if he owned the place. The light was better here than it had been in his hotel suite that first night. His six-pack abs were rigid below his sculpted pecs. His shoulders were broad, his biceps defined, and I saw he had an abstract blackwork tattoo on his left shoulder.

I wondered why I hadn't noticed it last night.

Our gazes locked, and my stress level spiked.

I rocked to my feet.

"Let's swim," I said to Brooklyn.

"In the water?" she asked, frowning as she looked my way from behind her sunglasses.

"Yes, in the water."

"It's cold in there."

"I'm hot."

"I'm not."

"Come on." I took her hand and pulled her to her feet.

"Whoa—"

"We need some exercise."

"Hey," Max greeted us all as he walked up.

"We're going swimming," I said to no one in particular.

"It looks that way," Colton said on a laugh.

I tossed my cover-up onto the lounger, catching Max's appreciative gaze as he took in my new swimsuit.

"Hi, Layla," he said.

"Hi." I gave him the shortest possible answer, then I headed for the pool, Brooklyn in tow.

"What is wrong with you?" she asked.

I sat down on the edge and dangled my feet in the water. It did feel cold, but I wasn't about to let that stop me. I slipped into the shallow end, the water coming to my waist.

"We need to talk," I said.

"We can't do that on dry land?" But she came into the water with me.

My gaze drifted to Max for a second, and I found him staring.

I dunked down to my neck to cover up a little.

"You're stuck to Colton like glue," I said.

"He's worth sticking to."

"James," I said. "Remember James."

Brooklyn's expression sobered. "I do."

I pushed backward, partly to get into the deeper water and partly to get farther away from Colton and Max. My body was starting to get used to the water temperature, and it felt rather good.

"You need to look at the big picture," I said.

"I'm looking at the long picture, the rest-of-my-life long picture."

"You only just met this guy." I had to admit, Colton didn't seem awful.

He hadn't done anything to justify my dislike of him. I hated what he was doing, but I didn't hate who he was. He was likely a decent guy, but Brooklyn was taken. She and James had a history and plans and a deep, abiding respect.

"I told you how I feel," she said, looking disappointed in me.

I felt a sliver of guilt. How she felt was wrong, but I couldn't figure out how to make her see that.

I moved a little closer to her. "I'm afraid you'll wake up one morning and realize this has all been a fantasy. This—" I gestured around the lavish pool deck and the hotel behind us "—isn't real. It's *Vegas*, for goodness sake."

"My feelings have nothing to do with Vegas."

I didn't believe her. But my wandering gaze landed on Max again. A man in a business suit had stopped by their loungers to talk.

"Exactly how often do they stay here?" I asked Brooklyn.

"Colton?" Brooklyn said.

"And Max. I'm assuming they must work together. They seem to know everyone."

"Everyone here?" she asked.

"Yes, here." Where else would I mean?

"I think they know most of the staff. They think it's important to pay attention to the people."

She had me confused. Max and Colton paid attention to the staff members of a hotel where they did business?

"Why?" I asked.

"Why what?"

"Why would they make such a big deal about getting to know the hotel staff?"

"It's good management."

"What do they manage?"

Brooklyn's brow furrowed in a way that told me I was talking nonsense.

"The hotel," she said.

Reality dawned on me. It had been staring me in the face. My attention shot back to Max. "They manage the hotel? *This* hotel?"

"They own this hotel. And they own the Archway Hotel. Well, their family does. And about eight others across the country."

I blinked. Then I blinked again. "Wait…what?"

"Why did you think your room rate was so low?"

"I don't know. Max said it was a corporate thing."

"It is a corporate thing. In this case, it's a family corporate thing."

I felt like a fool. Who gave out a rate more than ninety percent off? Nobody, that was who.

Then I thought about James. How was James going to compete with this? He had a good job. And as far as I knew he'd made some decent investments. He was well on his way, but he wasn't a multimillionaire, or a billionaire, or whatever it was that Colton was.

James couldn't offer Brooklyn free, unlimited room service, spa privileges or clothes-shopping sprees in iconic cities around the country. I didn't think Brooklyn was a gold digger—far from it. She had an authentic system of values that she lived by.

Still…

I took another moment to look around.

This was pretty heady stuff.

"I'm not interested in Colton's money," Brooklyn said, sounding annoyed.

"I didn't say—"

"I can see what you're thinking."

"That's *not* what I'm thinking."

"Then what are you thinking?"

I struggled to mentally compose a response.

"If you're editing your words, you're not being honest," Brooklyn said.

She was right. I owed it to her and to James to be bluntly honest. "You're breaking my brother's heart."

She looked like she might tear up. "I'm going to break his heart either way."

"Not if you change your mind."

If she would only come to her senses, we could fix this, it could all go away, and she and James would be happy, like they were meant to be.

"I won't change my mind," she said.

"You don't know that. That's the thing about changing your mind, you think something new. You think something different than you think right now, even if you're not expecting it. That's why they call it change."

She gave a sad shake of her head.

I took her hands in mine. "At least try. For me. Please. At least try."

"Okay," she said. "I won't get locked into a decision. I'll think about it a bit more."

"Good." I felt way better. At least this was the first step.

I woke up suddenly at 7:00 a.m., sitting bolt upright in my bed.

Worry over Brooklyn had kept me tossing and turning last night. Plus, the worry had been interspersed with guilt.

I'd never slept with a man and not talked it over with Brooklyn—often before, always after. And there was one time when she'd texted me during the kissing.

It was before our clothes came off, so technically not during sex. But I had answered the text to tell her the date was going well. That was true friendship.

And now, when my sex life impacted her most, I wasn't even sharing. The guilt sucked. But what had me throwing back the covers this morning was fear.

Max could have talked to Colton last night. He might have talked about him and me. He might have told Colton he'd had a one-night stand with Brooklyn's best friend, Layla. It would be a logical thing to do. It was certainly an interesting twist to the situation. It would be weird if Max hadn't mentioned it to Colton.

And if Max had told Colton, then it followed that Colton would tell Brooklyn. Then Brooklyn would know I lied, or omitted, or whatever you technically called it when a friend kept a highly significant piece of information from another friend.

The first friend should feel terrible, and the second friend would be furious. And the first friend had better come up with a rational and sincere apology.

And I would.

But first I had to find out everything Max had told Colton.

My phone rang and I grabbed for it. It was a long shot, but I hoped it was Max.

It was James.

I shifted my weight back onto the bed and reluctantly answered.

"Hi, James."

"You need to shut this down." His words were a punch to my stomach.

I had no idea how he knew what was going on. My first fear was that I had somehow given away Brooklyn's secret.

"Uh…" I struggled to come up with a response.

"I know how much you love hanging out with Brooklyn."

"I do." My heart rate steadied just a little bit, and I told myself to breathe.

"But I need her back. I need her back now, Layla. So whatever fun you two have cooked up there in Vegas, it has to stop."

"We will be back," I said.

"When?"

"Soon. Really soon. Just a few more…" I wanted to say hours, but I feared it could be days.

"It's irresponsible," he said, sounding annoyed.

"I've met a guy," I blurted out. It was the first excuse that popped into my mind. "And, well… I just need a bit of time."

"And Brooklyn to hold your hand?" James didn't sound any happier about that.

"You know I trust her."

"You lean on her too much."

"I know." I shook my head at the irony.

"Is she there?" he asked. "I tried her phone, but she must have let the battery run out again."

"Service is spotty in the hotel," I lied. "She's probably in the gym. She wants her wedding dress to fit. I mean, I know you haven't seen it or anything, but it's—"

"Don't tell me anything about the wedding dress! Brooklyn will flip out."

"Right. Yes. Of course. She's, uh, in the gym, I guess."

"You have to stop messing around, Layla."

"I will."

"I mean it. You might be her best friend, but I'm going to be her husband. And we've got a thousand details to take care of here."

"I know. I'll get her home. I promise."

He muttered something that might have been goodbye or a rare swear word. But at least he ended the call.

I breathed a sigh of relief.

It was short-lived when I remembered the problem I had with Max. I didn't have his phone number, but I knew his hotel suite.

Putting James out of my mind, I tossed on my jeans and a shirt, shoved my feet into my new sandals, finger-combed my hair and marched down the hall to the elevator.

It wasn't until I'd rapped at his door and was standing there waiting that I questioned my actions. What was he going to think of me showing up like this? He might not even be out of bed yet. I should have thought this through. Normally, I would have thought this through. But Max seemed to short-circuit the logical pathways of my left brain stem.

Reengaging them, I looked to the right and to the left, considering the option of abandoning my plan and rushing back down the hallway. But it was a long hallway. And if he opened the door and saw me running away, I'd feel even more mortified than I did just being here.

I stood my ground, hoping against hope that he hadn't heard the knock, hoping he was asleep, or maybe already at breakfast. He could be an early riser. He seemed like an early riser. Maybe he'd gone to the gym.

I pictured him at a rowing machine, shirt off, wearing black shorts like the black bathing trunks he'd worn at the pool yesterday. He'd looked hot, more than hot—cover-model hot. And not a cover model for a men's fashion magazine, a cover model for a magazine called *Muscle Monthly* or *Freak Fitness*.

The door opened.

It was obvious he was surprised to see me. His expression turned from surprised to curious, then to interested, then to sexy hopeful.

I was making the absolutely wrong impression. I wasn't here for an early morning roll in the sheets.

"Did you say anything?" I blurted out.

His face went back to puzzled again. "I'm going to need some context here, maybe a proper noun. Say anything about what?"

"About us, about you and me."

"What about you and me?"

I rolled my eyes. Aside from our one-night stand, was there anything else about us that was gossip worthy?

I was adept at sarcasm. "That we *ate a chocolate soufflé*."

"No." Amusement came into his eyes, like he thought this was all good and funny. "Well, the waiter and the chef knew, maybe a few of the kitchen staff. Why? Are you counting calories?"

"Don't be a jerk."

"Are you in some kind of strict diet club?"

My pride took a reflexive hit. "Do I look like I should be in a diet club?"

"No. And I think we can trust the cooking staff to keep our deep dark secrets."

"I mean the sex, Max."

"No kidding."

"Did you tell anyone? Did you tell Colton we slept together?"

"No."

My shoulders slumped in relief.

"I take it you didn't tell Brooklyn," Max said.

"No. I mean not yet. It's not like it's a secret."

"Sure. I can tell that by the way you're acting right now."

"It's not that I'm not going to tell her. I'm just thinking about the timing. I want to get it right. And there was a lot going on yesterday."

"Do you want some coffee?"

I did. "No thanks."

He stood to one side. "Come in and have some coffee. We'll get our stories straight."

"There's no story to get straight. I'm not planning to lie to Brooklyn."

The coffee sure did smell good.

"How about you tell me what you want me to say and not to say, and I'll stick to that."

A door opened farther down the hallway, and I realized that I wasn't keen on standing outside Max's suite looking like I'd just rolled out of bed, which I had, just not his bed.

"Okay," I said, heading inside. "I'll take some coffee."

"Great." He shut the door behind me.

The drapes were open, letting the morning sun into the big living room. It was neat as a pin, with a fresh floral arrangement on the coffee table and a silver coffee service on the dining table. Two cream-colored sofas faced each other, with two taupe leather armchairs at one end, positioned toward the glass French doors.

I hadn't noticed these details the night I'd been here, but the pastel abstracts and mosaic-tile wall features and the huge gas fireplace made the room look far more homey than a regular hotel suite. And it looked like there was a second bedroom and bathroom down a short hallway. It was truly huge.

"Do you stay here a lot?" I asked.

"When I'm here in Vegas," he said. "A few days a month, usually, but sometimes longer."

I could hear him pouring me a cup of coffee. "It's nice," I said, continuing to gaze around the room and at the pretty garden outside.

"Cream or sugar?" he asked.

"Both, please."

"Sweet and smooth," he said. "More than just coffee."

I turned to frown at his insinuation.

He grinned unrepentantly.

I refused to buy in, putting on the judgmental school-marm face that worked on my ninth graders. "Brooklyn told me you own the place."

He erased the grin. "My family owns a few hotels. It's not a chain, each is independently designed and run according to the market."

"You deliberately kept that from me."

He held the cup out to me. "Guilty."

"Why keep it secret?"

"I'm sure you can guess. It's the same reason I don't tell anyone right away. I didn't want to color your impression of me."

I moved closer to him and accepted the cup of coffee he was offering. "You think being überwealthy would make me like you less?"

"I'm not überwealthy."

I made a show of looking around the room. "Right. My mistake."

"*This* is why I didn't say anything."

"You do know with some women you're *more* not *less* likely to get lucky if they know you're rich."

"I wasn't thinking about getting lucky with you."

"Well, you did." I maybe should have been embarrassed about that. But I wasn't, not really.

Making love with Max had seemed so natural and wonderful at the time. Even looking back, I didn't regret it. I missed it.

He pulled out one of the dining chairs, the invitation implicit for me to sit down. It was the same spot where I'd sat while we ate the soufflé.

His coffee was now at the end of the rectangular table, the same spot he'd taken that night.

I sat.

"Muffin?" he asked, pointing to a basket as he took his seat.

They were plump and grainy, dotted with blueberries. On a tray beside the muffins were little pots of jam, cream cheese and butter.

I didn't see why I should try to resist.

I put one on a side plate and cut it in half, planning to smear it with cream cheese.

"I liked you," Max said. "I was thinking I wanted to get to know you better."

"You definitely did that."

"I don't want you to feel bad about it."

"I don't feel bad about it. And you don't have to dress it up. It was what it was." I spread some cream cheese on half of the muffin. "Plus, you bought me dinner, then a really great soufflé, twice on the soufflé, and now these wonderful muffins."

"Are you obsessed with food?"

"Not normally. But I need to look good in a very fitted bridesmaid dress less than two weeks from now…" I pictured my dress and Brooklyn's dress, and James, and then Colton. "Well, you know, maybe."

I set down the muffin, untouched, wondering if I was stress eating and if I should stop.

"Eat," Max said. "You have to keep up your strength."

"I'm hardly wasting away." The food at the Canterbury Sands was arguably the best in the country.

"Taste," he said and took a bite of his own muffin.

He'd gone with the orange marmalade, which would have been my second choice.

I took a bite of mine.

The muffin was fantastic. I washed it down with a sip of equally fantastic coffee.

"When are you going to tell her?" Max asked.

I took it to mean he was itching to tell Colton about us.

"Today," I said. "I'll let you know when you're clear to talk."

He shrugged. "I'm not going to talk."

"I thought you wanted to tell Colton."

"Why would I tell Colton?"

"You're his brother. I assumed you shared that kind of thing."

Max gave a little smile. "Not since we were teenagers."

I didn't know why I found that surprising. I hadn't really considered what men shared about their sex lives. I guess I'd assumed they were pretty much the same as women. We shared all the time.

Sex was interesting, and confusing, and impactful. I couldn't imagine keeping it all to myself.

"Even under these—" I hesitated over my words "—unusual circumstances?"

"Do you *want* me to tell Colton?"

"No."

"Do you think it will help anything if he knows?"

"It won't help if either of them knows. It sure won't help if Brooklyn knows. It'll distract her. She'll figure I like you. And if I like you, she'll think there's a chance I might come to like Colton, too. And I'm not going to like Colton because that would be betraying my brother. Nothing is going to change that."

"Is she wrong?" Max asked with a funny expression on his face.

I was confused. I thought I'd been clear. "Wrong?"

"Do you *not* like me?"

I realized how my words had sounded. I felt bad about that. "I never would have slept with you if I didn't like you."

"So that's a yes." There was a vulnerability in the question.

I found my gaze trapped by his. "That's a yes, Max. I like you."

He put his hand over mine.

It felt like a switch had been flipped, a circuit completed, like what should have been two had become one. My blood rushed through my veins, upping my heart rate, flushing my skin to a tingle and clouding the logical resources of my brain.

"Layla," he whispered. His thumb stroked my palm.

"I don't..." I couldn't finish the sentence. I didn't want to lie. "We can't," I said instead.

"What would it hurt?"

"It's already too complicated." Even as I spoke, I was leaning toward him.

"I wish I could take that as a yes," he said.

"I wish I could say yes," I told him honestly.

He withdrew his hand, and I regretted my refusal. I could have said yes. I should have said yes. The world would hardly come to a screeching halt if I said yes to him...again.

But he stood up and drew back. He finished the last of his coffee and set the cup on the table with finality. It was obviously time for me to go.

"Thank you," I said.

I wasn't sure if I meant for the coffee, the muffin, for keeping quiet about our lovemaking, or for so easily accepting my refusal to repeat it. I supposed it applied to all of it. Each of those things was considerate.

"Thank you," I said again as I came to my feet.

"No problem." But his voice was tight.

I'd either disappointed him or upset him—maybe both, probably both. I hadn't meant to blow hot and cold, but that was what I'd done.

I headed for the door before I could make the situation any worse.

Six

Later that morning I convinced Brooklyn to take a walk with me on the Strip. I had to get out of the hotel for a while.

"We're going to sweat," she said as we cleared the hotel driveway and started along the crowded sidewalk.

I could already feel the intense heat of the sun on my head. I was glad I'd slathered some of the hotel's suntan lotion on my neck and arms.

"Look there," I said, pointing to a souvenir display in an open storefront. "Let's cover our heads."

The store was selling bright pink hats with glittering red letters that said Love Las Vegas. While I didn't completely agree with the sentiment, the colors were fun and I did want to avoid heatstroke.

We paid the inflated price and plopped them on our heads.

"Slushy?" she asked as we passed another stall.

"Absolutely." I was thirsty, and the drinks definitely looked refreshing.

She linked her arm with mine. "With tequila or without?"

"It's eleven o'clock in the morning."

"It's Vegas."

"It's still too early for tequila."

"Vodka then." Brooklyn laughed.

"I was thinking watermelon and maybe some of the blueberry."

The slush dispensers displayed their bright-colored wares through the windows of the machines. It was self-serve, so a person could customize their own drink.

"Pineapple," Brooklyn said. "Or maybe cola. I could go for a little caffeine."

"Late night?" I asked. Then I regretted the question. I sure didn't want to hear the details of Brooklyn's night with Colton.

"We talked and talked," she said.

I was grateful for her discretion.

"What size do you want?" I chose a medium plastic cup for myself.

Brooklyn took the same.

She mixed cola with lemon then mocked me as I made a rainbow out of blueberry, watermelon and peach.

It felt like old times as we headed down the Strip sipping our drinks.

We came across a woman in a crocheted bathing suit with a brown python draped around her neck.

"Is that real?" I asked.

It moved, and I knew it was. I jumped to the opposite side of Brooklyn, who laughed at me.

"Why is she doing that?" I squeaked.

Then I noticed other people wearing various snakes around their necks. Revulsion crept up my spine. Yuck.

"People pay for the pictures," Brooklyn said.

"Why?"

"It's Vegas," she said with a bored nonchalance and dismissive wave, acting like a local.

"You've been here all of *two days*," I pointed out.

We made it past the snake people. I couldn't stop myself from glancing behind us to make sure none of the slithery creatures were sneaking up.

"I've had the tour," she said. "It's a really wild place."

"I'll say." I shuddered as I gave a final thought to the snakes.

The last thing in the world I wanted was to feel one of them around my neck. Never mind pay for the privilege, never mind capture my look of horror for posterity and possible internet posts.

If for no other reason, I was a high school teacher. I had a certain dignity to maintain.

Droplets of water were condensing on my slushy. I switched the cup to my left hand and shook my right one dry.

We passed families, couples and gaudily dressed actors, hawkers handing out flyers, and sellers of every imaginable tourist trinket.

It took me six blocks to work up my courage. "You asked me about Max yesterday," I said as we stopped for a light at an intersection.

The crowd surged around us.

"I like him," Brooklyn said. "I guess I'm predisposed to like him, since he's a lot like Colton." She gave a little laugh. "Then again, he's a lot not like Colton, too."

The light changed, and we started walking, propelled along with the crowd as I framed and discarded wording inside my head.

"It must be weird being a twin," she said.

"I slept with Max," I blurted out.

Brooklyn stopped dead in the middle of the intersection.

I stopped, too, and a woman with two little girls banged into the back of me. "Sorry," I said to the woman.

She frowned at me.

"Seriously?" Brooklyn asked.

"Keep walking," I said.

"When? Why? How?"

I grabbed her arm and tugged her along. "The usual way."

"Ha, ha. Very funny. *When* did this happen?"

"I couldn't find you the night I got here. I looked all over for you. I staked out the lobby for hours and hours. You ignored my texts. You wouldn't answer your phone."

"So your solution was to sleep with Max?"

"I wouldn't have even been with Max if I'd been able to find you."

"So you're saying it's my fault."

"Yes. No. It's not your fault. You were, however, a contributing factor."

"You slept with Max." There was a note of wonder in Brooklyn's voice, a note of happy wonder.

"Oh, no, you don't," I said.

"Don't what?"

"Start picturing… I don't know—double dates or something."

It was clear she was doing exactly what I would have done in her shoes.

"I wasn't picturing that," she said.

"I'm on *James's* side."

We stopped for another light.

"You like Max?" Brooklyn asked.

"Yes, I like Max." There was no point in denying it. Brooklyn knew perfectly well that I wouldn't sleep with a guy unless I liked him a lot.

"He's also very hot," I said, feeling like I needed more justification for my actions. It wasn't like I slept with every guy I liked.

"So is Colton."

Her words gave me pause. I knew Colton was a good-looking man. He was identical to Max, after all. But he wasn't hot like Max, at least not to me. There were differences in their expressions and their mannerisms, and definitely in their perspectives.

I couldn't see Max dating an engaged woman.

I wasn't sure why I felt that way, but I did. Maybe it was the way he'd reacted when I'd asked him if he was married. He was clearly appalled by the thought of breaking his marriage vows.

An engagement might not be a vow. But it was a promise. It was a promise that deserved to be kept.

We started walking again. The crowds thinned as the quirky storefronts turned to higher-end businesses.

"Where is this all coming from?" I asked her. "You were so happy. You were both so excited to get married."

She sipped her drink through the straw.

I figured she was composing an answer. I have to admit, if I was her, I'd have had that answer all thought up by now.

"It wasn't one single thing," she said. "I was excited about the wedding, and I was happy about settling everything, becoming an official member of your family after all those years. But then we started talking about kids."

"I'm sure James will wait on the kids." I was positive he would. "You must not have made it clear how much waiting meant to you."

Brooklyn shook her head.

She spotted a trash bin and dropped the remains of her drink.

I did the same.

"It's not just the kids," she said.

I had to admit, I didn't think that could be the only reason.

"I was living a fantasy," she said.

"That's not a bad thing. It's a good thing. What woman wouldn't want to live out her fantasy of marrying such a fantastic guy?"

"It's nothing against James, you know."

I found that pretty hard to believe. Brooklyn was trying to replace my brother with another man. How could that be anything *but* a slight against James?

"Prewedding jitters really are a thing," I said.

At least people sure talked about them a lot. And I could easily see how a guy like Colton might sweep an uncertain Brooklyn off her feet.

He was exotic, handsome and wealthy. It seemed like he could give her anything she wanted. James could come off as staid by comparison.

"I was thinking this before I even met Colton," she said.

"You weren't canceling the wedding before you met Colton."

"I was silently panicking."

"Jitters," I repeated. "I bet lots of brides feel that way."

Brooklyn gave a heavy sigh of what I took to be frustration with my attitude.

"You promised you wouldn't make a quick decision," I reminded her.

It was clear that if Brooklyn decided now, James would come out on the losing end of that decision.

"You don't want to do anything you'll regret," I said. "Don't do anything you can't take back." I could hear the pleading tone in my voice. I wasn't particularly proud of that, but at the same time, I couldn't help wondering if it would work.

"I know," she said.

"Maybe you should talk to James about this."

Her eyes got really big. "Are you kidding?"

Hearing the words out loud made me realize it wasn't one of my best ideas.

"Are you *kidding*?" she repeated. "How exactly do you see that conversation going?"

"I don't suppose it would go well," I admitted.

"Darn straight it wouldn't go well."

I watched her stricken expression, at how worried she looked. Reality seemed to be finally settling in. She was talking about leaving James, about tossing away their years together, their plans and dreams on a whim.

"Do you think it's a sign?" I asked.

"Do I think what's a sign?"

"How afraid you are to talk to James. It could be a sign you're not ready to leave him."

Brooklyn fell silent, obviously giving my words some thought.

I started to hope.

I couldn't imagine a world in which Brooklyn wasn't with James. The planet would be out of kilter, off its axis.

I already pictured my nieces and nephews with James's eyes or Brooklyn's hair. They might want to stop after two, but I was thinking three or four would be better. They were both terrific with kids. I could imagine summer picnics and Christmas mornings, ballet classes or Little League.

My future plans included James and Brooklyn's happy family. They did not include Brooklyn bopping from Las Vegas to San Francisco to New York City with some stranger.

I tried to pretend Brooklyn hadn't ditched me. I knew that was exactly what had happened, and it hurt my pride to think she'd rather spend time with Colton than me.

I hadn't felt that way about James. It never seemed like Brooklyn was giving up time with me to spend it with him. She and I still had plenty of time together. If I had a boyfriend, we'd double date. When we were teenagers, Brooklyn was usually at our house, so I was with them more often than not. And when I wasn't in a relationship, which was pretty often, we'd do more group activities than one-on-one dating.

Was it odd that James and Brooklyn hadn't spent all that much time alone?

Under the circumstances, I didn't really want to ask myself if that was normal. It could easily be normal. It wasn't a sign of anything negative. I had to be reengineering the past, seeing problems where they didn't even exist.

I didn't want to spend any extra money while I was here, so I'd decided the hotel's courtyard lagoon pool was a better choice than an overpriced lunch. It cost me nothing to find a lounger under a palm tree, help myself to the complimentary towels and suntan lotion, and say yes to the offer of ice water from a friendly pool attendant.

It was warm, and I was comfortable. I'd even found a half-finished novel buried in an app on my phone. It was a comedy sleuth story, lightweight enough that I picked up the plot in a couple of pages. It was exactly what I needed to distract me.

"Enjoying the sunshine?" Max's voice alerted me to his approach before I heard his footsteps above the laughter of the children in the pool.

I looked up and was struck all over again by his great looks. He was wearing a white dress shirt with the sleeves rolled up over a pair of casual gray slacks. He didn't exactly look like he was working. He didn't exactly look like he was relaxing, either.

"What is it you do around here?" I asked as the question popped into my mind.

"In what way?"

"What's your job? When you spend time at one of your hotels, what do you do? I'm assuming they each have a general manager, since you and—" I caught myself.

"His name is Colton."

"I know that." I took a beat. Saying his name always seemed to implicitly acknowledge his relationship with Brooklyn. But I couldn't exactly use "he who shall not be named" when I was talking to his twin brother.

I tried again. "Since you and Colton don't seemed to be assigned to a specific hotel."

Max looked amused, his eyes lighting in a way that both attracted and annoyed me. I hated that he could so effortlessly evoke an emotional reaction in me. I wasn't an emotional person. I was a logical person. And it wasn't logical for me to indulge in this attraction.

He sat down sideways on the lounger next to mine.

"We do a bunch of things," he said.

"Inspect the troops?" It sounded silly after I said it.

But Max flashed a grin, like he thought it was funny. "And the equipment, and the building. We check in with the general manager and the department managers to see how things are running. We look at financial reports, guest response amalgamations, troubleshoot, that sort of thing."

"What kind of trouble do you find?"

"It's a constant fight to stay ahead of upgrading. Sometimes a restaurant has run its course, people's tastes and trends change and we need to refresh decor and menus. There are mechanical breakdowns, human-resources issues—we once found fraud."

"Someone was stealing from you?"

"They were."

My curiosity was piqued. It wasn't what I'd expected him to say, and I couldn't help but wonder about the details of the crime. "Interesting. I'm good when it comes to numbers."

"Meaning you could help discover fraud or help perpetrate fraud?"

"Depends on the circumstances. You have a fraud that needs perpetrating?"

"Not at the moment, you know, since I'd be stealing my own money. But I'll keep you in mind in case anything comes up."

"I've always wanted to moonlight," I said.

He chuckled.

"So you caught them?" I asked on a more serious note.

"Two employees were in on it. One was cooking the books. The other was signing off on bogus expenses. Turned out they were having an affair and had cooked up a plan to take the money and move to the Caribbean." Max paused. "Instead they moved to Nevada State Prison."

His tone and expression made me smile.

I was about to express my surprise that his job involved fighting crime, when my phone rang.

I picked it up from the little rattan table, expecting Brooklyn. But it was James's number that showed on the screen.

I felt a lurch of guilt for joking around with Max. But I put on a cheerful tone as I answered. "Hey, how's it going in Seattle?"

"Are you with Brooklyn?" James asked straight away.

I hesitated for less than a second. "Yes. She's here."

She was here somewhere, I reasoned, either in the hotel or in the greater Las Vegas area.

"Please put her on the phone."

"Why? Is something wrong? Can I help?" I hoped James wouldn't catch on to my stalling.

"Nothing is wrong. I'd like to talk to my fiancée."

"Did you call her phone?"

"Of course I called her phone. Just like I did this morning. Ask her if it's even turned on."

"I, uh, can't." My mind scrambled for an answer to his inevitable next question.

"Why not?"

"She's not exactly right here, right now." Inspiration was right in front of me. "She's in the pool." And once I'd given over to outright lies, my mouth seemed to go for it. "Brooklyn," I called out in a loud voice.

Max gave me a look that said he knew exactly what I was doing. I ignored him. "James is on the phone," I called to the fictitious Brooklyn.

I waited a moment.

"Can she call you back?" I asked James.

"Tell her to get out of the pool."

"She's...playing volleyball. It's a close game. She doesn't want to let down her team." Okay, I was starting to amaze myself. Not only was I breaking my own moral code, but it also turned out I was pretty good at it.

"This is getting out of hand," James said with obvious frustration.

"We're just cutting loose," I said, telling myself it was closer to the truth. "We're having some extra girl time before the wedding. You had a bachelor party."

"The bachelor party lasted six hours."

"So we're less efficient. I'll get her to call you back."

"Don't bother."

My stomach sank, thinking James somehow knew what was going on.

"Why not?" I asked. I could hear the trepidation in my own tone.

"Because I'm not waiting. I'm getting the next plane."

"Don't do that," I said too fast.

I could feel James gathering himself across the phone line. "And why not?"

I avoided Max's gaze. "I met a guy."

"So you said this morning."

"I know. But it really is maybe a thing. And Brooklyn's being my wingman. You know how worried she's been about me being lonely now that you're getting married."

James was silent for a second. "That's true."

His answer took me back. Brooklyn wasn't worried about me. *Was* she worried about me? Why would she worry about me? I wasn't lonely. There absolutely was nothing for her to worry about.

Well, not when it came to her marrying James, anyway. When it came to Colton, the story was completely different. In that, she ought to be very worried about my reaction to that.

Max was peering at me.

James was silent.

I recovered my surprise and told myself to take the win.

"Great," I said to James. "Thanks. It'll only be a little bit longer."

"Hurry up," he said.

"I will," I promised.

He muttered something unintelligible again, then the line went dead.

I lowered my phone.

"That was interesting," Max said.

"You could have given me some privacy," I pointed out.

"I could have," he agreed. "I take it I'm the guy—the guy that's maybe a thing?"

"It's not you. It's not anybody. There is no guy. It was a story." I told myself it was for a good cause. In this particular scenario the end more than justified the means.

"I think the word you're looking for is *lie*," Max said.

I flashed him a glare. He barely knew me, and here he was judging away. He was the one in the wrong. Well, his brother was the one in the wrong.

Many people were in the wrong, and I was trying to make it right…by doing something underhanded. Yeah, I got that.

"Come out with me," Max said.

I didn't understand.

"Let's go on a date. That way your lie won't be as much of a lie, and you'll feel better about it."

"I don't feel bad about it," I said.

His grin went broad. "You should see your face. It's killing you."

"I'm perfectly fine."

He got to his feet. "You are the most painfully honest person. I should definitely offer you a job in our accounting division."

"I already have a job." For some reason I felt the need to remind him, though it was irrelevant to the conversation.

"Let's go," he said.

"To the accounting office?"

How far was he planning to carry the joke?

"On our date."

"Now?" Not that I had said yes. Not that I was planning to say yes. Going forward, I was keeping my distance from Max, not dating him.

"Yes, now. Let's make you honest. You'll feel better, I promise."

"You have no idea what will make me feel better."

"A bottle of Crepe Falls Reserve says I will." He held his hand out to me.

I wanted to take it, and I had to stop myself from reaching up. And it had nothing to do with my competitive instincts or with a newfound weakness for Crepe Falls Reserve.

"There's a hot-air balloon tour this afternoon. It's really great. It takes you to the rim of the Grand Canyon," Max said.

I found myself hesitating—a hot-air balloon tour instead of waiting around for Brooklyn?

Brooklyn pitied me. She was worried about me. She probably thought I was lonely without her.

I didn't like to think that I might be lonely without her.

I sure wouldn't be lonely while floating over the Grand Canyon. I had to admit, a tour like that sounded marvelous. It sounded downright bucket-list marvelous.

Max wiggled his hand. "Come on, Layla. What've you got to lose?"

"A bottle of Crepe Falls Reserve, apparently," I said.

"That's the spirit."

Brooklyn didn't need to worry about me. I could take care of myself.

In fact, maybe I'd back off on pressing her to make the right decision. The novelty of Colton could easily fade, would most likely fade. But they needed time together—all alone together, with no distractions and nothing else to do but stare at each other.

That's what it would take for Brooklyn to get over Colton.

Taking the adventure of a lifetime with Max might just be the best way to help James. I wasn't even deluding myself. I truly believed it was worth a shot.

"I can't be gone too long," I said.

"I'll have you back by dinner."

* * *

Floating near the rim of the Grand Canyon, I was in awe. The view of the red-rock cliffs was outstanding. The sky was crisp blue, and the mottled scrub of green cacti went on and on.

I was also afraid—not of the height. What scared me was the fun. I was having a whole lot of fun with Max on this exotic, expensive date.

The hot-air balloon ride was exhilarating on its own. But it had started with a twenty-minute helicopter flight from Vegas over Lake Mead to the balloon-launch site. There we were greeted by a professional tour guide dressed in a suit and tie, and an obviously knowledgeable balloon pilot named Rick, who briefed us on safety.

They gave us jackets in case we got cold, showed us how to work on the oxygen masks in case we went over 10,000 feet and then we had a toast with champagne before we left the ground.

The champagne was chilled, and it was high-end, and it wasn't served in plastic cups like you might expect at a picnic site. Oh, no, nothing that tacky. We were handed crystal flutes to ensure nothing marred the opulence of our experience.

With the colorful balloon above us, we soared past red-rock cliffs.

Max and I gazed out at the gnarled trees, the towering saguaro cactuses and the flashes of delicate, colored flowers that grew in bunches on the desert floor. A hawk glided above us and a coyote trotted below.

Rick, the pilot, was behind us, controlling the burner.

"Tell me about your brother," Max said.

The question put me on my guard. "Why?"

"I've been thinking about him since your phone call."

I really didn't want to think about that phone call. I

didn't want to think about my dishonesty. I wanted to think about the beautiful desert rolling out in front of us.

"It's easy for me to see Colton's side in this," Max said, either not noticing my silence or not caring. "He and Brooklyn seem good together, and—"

"James and Brooklyn are *way* better together."

"I'm not saying they're not."

I pressed my point. "What they have is solid and real."

"It may well be."

I was determined to argue, but Max wasn't really arguing back. That annoyed me, but I wasn't exactly sure how to counter it. How did you complain about someone not fighting with you?

We both fell silent. The wind blew against our faces as we glided. The roar of the burner ebbed and flowed.

"About your brother," he said.

"What?" I asked, exasperated that he wouldn't just let it lie. "Are you scoping out the competition for Colton?"

"No. I'm trying to understand both sides."

"Why would you want to do that?"

"Because it's a reasonable thing to do when there are two perspectives."

"You're hardly a neutral party."

He was pulling for his own brother, plain and simple. Not that I blamed him. I was sure pulling for James. But I felt like I had a stronger claim. Which I know sounds ridiculous. Brooklyn's feelings were her own, not mine or Max's or Colton's, or even James's. Still…

"I'm considering the wisdom of helping you," Max said.

"Helping me do what?"

"I think you may have a point."

I'm not a suspicious person, but this sounded too good to be true. "About what?"

The balloon basket lurched. I fell against Max, and he wrapped his arm firmly around me, steadying me.

I didn't want to like the feeling. I wasn't a maiden in distress. I didn't need a strong handsome man to keep me out of harm's way. It wasn't like I was about to fall.

Still, I didn't pull back.

I wasn't sure why.

Okay, I was sure why.

The rocky basket was an excuse to hug Max again without admitting what I was doing. Then again, I'd just admitted what I was doing, so it wasn't like I was fooling myself.

"Colton and Brooklyn just met," Max said. "It's possible what they feel won't last."

"Exactly!" I blurted.

The basket lurched, more suddenly this time, and the floor seemed to drop from beneath us.

My stomach dropped along with it.

Max twisted his head to look back at the pilot.

I could imagine his question was the same as mine—something along the lines of "what the heck?"

"Wind shear," Rick called out. The roar of the burner became constant. "I'm fighting a pretty strong downdraft."

I was about to ask if we were going to fall, when the floor stabilized, our descent growing more constant.

"That was exciting," I said to Max. I almost, but not quite, kept the tremble from my voice.

"That's one word for it," he said.

"Were you scared?" I asked.

"Not so far."

The basket was rapidly descending.

The roar increased, and I saw the pilot was using both of the burners.

I found myself mesmerized by the rising earth. If I had

to guess, I'd say we were a hundred feet above the sloped, tree-dotted hillside.

I wouldn't say we were plummeting, but we were falling faster than I wanted to hit the ground, that was for sure.

"There's a fifteen-second delay for the balloon to respond to the added heat," Rick told us.

"Are *you* scared?" I asked Rick.

He looked perfectly calm.

"We'll slow down in a moment," he told me. "We may make a hard landing."

"Is that a euphemism for *crash*?" I asked, not really sure that I wanted the answer.

"Landing," he assured me.

"Don't be scared," Max said.

"I'm not," I lied. I was getting scared now. The ground was only about fifty feet away.

"Feel that?" Rick asked.

Our rate of descent had definitely slowed down.

I heard him try his radio.

"Are you sending a Mayday?" I asked.

"I'm trying to raise a signal."

"There's no signal?" I was embarrassed at the little squeak at the end of my question. But I was starting to picture us stranded in the desert, injured by the fall, nobody knowing how to find us while we died of thirst or were attacked and eaten by coyotes.

Brooklyn tells me I get ahead of myself. She tells me that I love to play "worst-case scenario."

She's not wrong. I admit, I do do that. But in this case I figured I was playing "most likely case scenario." That was a completely different thing.

"We're being monitored on GPS," Max said, obviously guessing my worry. "They know where we are."

"I want to let them know we landed safely," Rick said.

I looked over the edge of the basket. There were trees directly beneath us, and we were closing in.

"We haven't landed safely," I pointed out.

"Once—"

A strong cross breeze gusted against us.

"Whoa," Rick said, shutting off the burners. "Hang on!"

Max plastered me to his stomach with one arm, gripping the edge of the basket with the other.

The basket caught on the branches of one of the trees. The branches snapped off and the balloon kept going.

Then we hit the next tree. This one had more strength and it held us in place. The wind buffeted the giant balloon, fighting with the tree for control of the basket.

"What is—" I began, but I didn't get to finish.

The basket tipped sideways. I cried out, but I was proud that I didn't actually scream.

My heart was pumping furiously as I grasped at the air, searching for something to hang on to.

Max's grip on me tightened as I almost slid out of the basket.

"Keep still. I've got you," he said.

Max kept us in place by holding on to the basket with one arm and me with the other.

I couldn't help but wonder how long he could do that.

Rick had been thrown, and he now hung from the lip of the basket, his feet kicking as he searched for a tree branch for support.

He seemed to find something. He breathed a sigh of relief and hoisted himself with his elbows, then his shoulders, farther into the basket.

"You okay?" Max asked him.

"Yes, you?" Rick asked.

"We're good," Max said.

"Sorry about the hard landing," he said.

I almost laughed. I assumed he was joking. "That felt like a crash."

"It's not a crash if you walk away," Rick said, keeping his tone light on purpose—no doubt.

"This is going to be interesting," Max said.

"Interesting?" I echoed with incredulity.

We were stuck in a tree with a ten-foot drop to the ground.

"We can do this," Max assured me.

I wanted to be brave. I wished with all my heart I could be brave. I didn't want to look like a coward in front of Max. But I didn't want to break my limbs, either.

The basket flexed beneath us, and my heart took a jump.

"Can you get your girlfriend down?" Rick asked.

I started to protest the title, but then I stopped. Under the circumstances, correcting Rick would be silly.

Max stretched out on his stomach, then he motioned to me. "Give me your hands."

I couldn't help glancing at the drop-off from the mouth of the basket. "What are you going to do?"

"If I hold you over the edge at arm's length, your feet will almost touch the ground."

"Almost?" I didn't really like the sound of that, never mind the idea of dangling in midair while Max lowered me.

What if he lost his grip? What if the basket tipped further and we both tumbled out? I'd break my legs and Max would break his neck.

Just then the wind gusted, catching the half-inflated balloon, lurching us against the tree.

"Do it now," Rick said.

"Take my hands," Max said.

I didn't hesitate anymore. Whatever courage I'd been looking for showed up in an instant. I skootched over and gave Max my hands.

He took me by the wrists.

"Hang on to me," he said.

I gripped his wrists the way he gripped mine.

"Slide backward," he told me. "Don't look down."

I decided that was very good advice. I settled my gaze on his.

He gave me a smile. "This is going to be easy."

"I don't believe you." But I was already inching back. Some primal part of my brain told me I had to act, I had to do exactly as he said to make sure we all got out of this without getting hurt.

"That's good," Max said as my feet dangled free.

I folded at the waist, then I wiggled back even more. As I reached the balance point, I took a breath and kept going.

Max's gaze remained locked with mine until I was dangling at his arm's length.

"It's about two feet to the ground," he told me. "Like jumping off a chair. Bend your knees when you land."

I was ready.

I nodded.

He let me drop.

Seven

We made it onto solid ground with nothing more than minor scrapes and bruises. Rick headed up the side of the hill with the radio to try to raise a signal. Meanwhile, Max sized up the trapped basket.

"It's not coming down," he said, coming over to where I was sitting on a smooth rock. "Not without help, anyway."

I was watching a moving shape on the horizon. "Is that a coyote?"

Max followed my gaze. "It is."

"Is it dangerous?"

"Only if you're a jackrabbit. It won't bother us."

"Are you sure?"

It was possible Max was lying to make me feel better. The animal had stopped now. It was staring right at us, and it looked hungry. There wasn't a lot of game out here in the desert. We probably looked delicious.

"What does your brother do for a living?" Max asked, sitting down next to me.

"He could have friends lurking out there."

"James?"

"The coyote."

I watched the nature channel. I knew coyotes traveled in packs. They might not be big, but a well-coordinated pack could take down a deer. I'd seen it happen, and it wasn't pretty.

"Is he a teacher like you?" Max asked. "Lawyer? Banker?"

"James is an economist."

The coyote put his nose to the ground and started toward us.

"Should we climb the tree?" I asked.

"Does he work for a government? A chamber of commerce? A Fortune 500?"

"A consulting firm."

Max seemed very calm. I decided to assume our lives weren't in imminent danger.

"I assume he's a good-looking man."

I took my gaze off the approaching coyote long enough to check Max's expression. That was an odd assumption.

"He's your brother," Max said. "The genetic odds seem to be in his favor."

The oblique compliment took me by surprise. I couldn't decide if I should thank him and seem conceited or let it slide and seem ungrateful.

Suddenly Max jumped to his feet and shouted, "Ha!"

The coyote startled about thirty feet away.

My insides froze with fear.

Max waved his arms. "Go on!"

The coyote twisted his body, turning away, but watched us over his shoulder as he trotted.

"Ha!" Max shouted again.

The coyote began to run.

"You said he wasn't dangerous." My voice had a definite shake to it.

"He's not."

"He was coming for us."

"He didn't know what we were. We're pretty far out in the desert right now. I doubt he sees a lot of people."

"He wanted to eat us." I was sure of that.

Coyotes were predators, and we were prey.

"He ran away," Max pointed out.

"You had to scare him away."

"I just let him know we were bigger than he is." Max sat back down and took my hand. "Relax. You're perfectly safe."

I gazed at the hill where the pilot had climbed. "What about Rick?"

"He'll be back soon."

"I hope he's okay." I wouldn't have wanted to be climbing around up that hill all by myself.

"What's the name of your brother's firm?"

"O'Neil Nybecker."

"That's a solid firm."

"He's a solid guy." I'd been bragging about my brother most of my life—except when I was really young, and except for those teenage years when he embarrassed me nearly to death. The rest of the time I accepted that he was an exceptional brother.

"Top of his class at UW," I said.

"Impressive," Max responded in an easy tone.

"His varsity four-man crew took silver in the nationals."

"Colton lettered in cross-country."

That wasn't exactly what I wanted to hear. "Is this a contest?"

"It's beginning to feel like one."

"You asked."

"I did," he agreed.

"What about you?" I found myself curious, thinking about what Max might have been like in college. "Did you run cross-country?"

"I played second base."

My interest was piqued. "I coach softball. Freshman and sophomore."

"Good for you."

"We all contribute to the extracurricular activities." I didn't want him to think I was bragging about some kind of extraordinary contribution to North Hill High. All the teachers were dedicated.

"Do you play?" he asked.

"I do. In a rec league. You?"

"Same."

There was something about his answer that projected a quiet confidence.

"You're really good, aren't you?"

"Lots of guys are better than me."

"No, they're not."

He smiled at that statement, but didn't answer.

"I knew it," I said.

"How long have James and Brooklyn been together?"

"Since high school. Even before that, really. Brooklyn's been my best friend forever."

"They have a lot in common?"

I thought about how to answer that. "Not everything. They're good foils for each other. James is solid and steady. Brooklyn is more impulsive, full of energy, great ideas and tons of fun. Together, they work."

"Do they fight?"

"Almost never."

"Do you find that odd?"

"I find it great. They've been around each other forever, and they've always gotten along."

"Do you think that could be the problem?"

I wasn't about to admit there was a problem.

I mean, I knew there was a problem. It was less than two weeks to the wedding.

Brooklyn was in Vegas hanging out with Colton instead of back in Seattle doing the final fitting of her wedding gown. But I wasn't ready to admit that to anyone but myself.

"There's no problem."

"Maybe they were too close. More like siblings than lovers."

"They're not siblings. They've been dating for years. Believe me, they know the difference." As I spoke, I couldn't help remembering Brooklyn saying she loved James, but she wasn't in love with James. At the time, it had struck me as a trivial distinction. I didn't even know what she meant.

"Okay," Max said with an air of finality.

"Okay what?"

"Okay, we'll do it your way."

"Do what? What are we doing?" I couldn't help but look around at the open desert and wonder if I'd missed something.

"We'll try to break them up. I'll help you."

I wasn't about to walk into that kind of a too-good-to-be-true offer. "Sure you will."

"I mean it. You could very well be right. The blush of their hormone high will wear off, and they could find that's all they ever really had."

"And Brooklyn's life would be ruined," I said, daring to consider Max might be serious. It would sure help for me to have him on my side. I'd rather it be an even battle than three on one. Plus, Max had the advantage of knowing Colton. That insider knowledge would definitely help me out.

If Max was serious.

I hoped he was serious.

I wasn't buying in without testing him. "Why would you help me?"

"I like you."

That seemed too simple. Also, it seemed unlikely. "You wouldn't betray your brother for some random woman."

"I don't consider you some random woman."

"I showed up randomly in your life two days ago."

"Three days ago, and it was more inevitable than random."

I guess I knew what he meant. First we saw each other in San Francisco. I wasn't about to ask if he'd felt something then, but I sure remembered the impact on me. Then there was the lobby lounge in Vegas, then dinner, then Brooklyn and Colton.

It did have an air of inevitability around it.

"It's still only three days," I said. "And he is your twin brother."

"And I don't want to see him make a mistake."

Now I had hope. "You think it's a mistake?"

"I give it fifty-fifty."

"I'd give it less than that."

"I've seen them together. They think it's real."

"They're wrong," I said.

"Do you want my help or not?"

"Yes. I do."

"Good. Rick's back."

I looked at the hillside and saw Rick coming our way. The sun was falling behind him, and the shadows were getting longer. We'd been away from the hotel for a long time. Brooklyn had to be wondering where I'd gone.

"Did you tell anyone we went up in the balloon?" I asked Max.

I hadn't texted Brooklyn. Mostly because I thought

we'd be back before she and Colton returned. And also because I didn't want her getting the impression I'd gone on a date with Max.

It was a fake date.

If it was an actual date, there'd have been intimacy—flirting, kissing and hugging and things like that.

As I rationalized, I couldn't help but remember being in his arms when the balloon went down. But that didn't count. I'd feared for my life. Any strong man's arms around me would have felt good.

"I didn't tell anyone," Max said.

"So they don't know where we are?"

"We can tell them all about it when we get back. It'll make a really good story."

"That you saved my life." I guess if I was Max, I'd be bragging, too.

"I didn't save your life." He paused. "Maybe your ankle. I probably saved you from a broken ankle."

"Thank you," I said.

He chuckled. "I wasn't fishing for that."

Rick grew closer. "Help is on the way!"

The helicopter that flew us out of the desert brought us all the way to the hotel.

It was my first and only time using a rooftop landing pad. I had to admit, I found it incredibly efficient. I could see why the superrich liked to travel that way. It sure beat fighting traffic in my Honda on Route 99.

I called Brooklyn from the express elevator.

It took a few rings, and she sounded breathless when she picked up. "Layla!"

I didn't want to imagine what I'd interrupted, and I didn't ask. "Hi."

"What time is it?"

"Just after six."

"I was going to call you earlier." Her words were rushed.

I realized then that she hadn't even noticed I was gone. There was no way that was good.

"But I got distracted," Brooklyn continued.

"James called," I said, hoping to shake her up a little.

She paused, as I'd hoped she would. Her tone turned cautious. "What did he want?"

The question struck me as ridiculous. "He wanted you. He wanted to know what was taking so long. He wanted to come here to see you."

Her voice went up an octave, the sound of panic creeping into it. "He can't do that."

"In fact, he can."

"I need more time, more time to think. Seeing him is going to mess me up."

I took pity on her. I don't know why, but I did. "He's not coming. I talked him out of it."

"Good." Brooklyn seemed to calm down. "That's good. You're the best."

"No, I'm not." I felt like a traitor.

"Where are you right now?" she asked.

"I'm in the hotel."

"I'll come and meet you."

I could hear in the phone that she was walking now. I was encouraged that she wanted to meet me right away. We needed to find somewhere to talk—not that I was exactly sure what more I could say. But I had to keep trying. I had to keep trying for as long as it took.

"Do you have plans tonight?" she asked.

What a nonsensical question. No, I didn't have plans tonight. She was my plans for as long as we were stuck in Vegas.

"I'm free," I said.

"Because, well, Colton has tickets to the Twenties Tangle."

Colton, Colton, Colton. I wanted to bang my head against the elevator.

"He's had the tickets for months," she said.

I didn't care if he'd had the tickets for years. "Can he not go alone?" I caught Max's quizzical gaze.

"It's a dance," Brooklyn said.

"You're going to a dance?"

Her world was falling apart around her, and she was going to a dance?

"The Twenties Tangle," Max said to me.

I gave him a glare of frustration.

"We found this supercool flapper dress," Brooklyn said.

I covered my phone. "Your brother needs to stop."

"Stop what?"

"It's all silver and black," Brooklyn said into my ear. "With lace and tassels and sequins. There's a rhinestone headband, and you should see the shoes."

"Buying Brooklyn's affections," I said to Max.

He moved closer, keeping his voice low. "With what?"

"A dress."

"A dress?" He looked puzzled. "I thought maybe some diamonds or a car."

I gave him a shove with my shoulder.

He didn't even budge.

"We need to talk," I said to Brooklyn. "We need to have a really good talk."

"The dress is in my room. Do you want to see it?"

"No, I don't want to see your dress."

"I have tickets," Max said to me. "We can go with them."

I covered my phone again. "That's your big plan to break them up? A double date?"

"You want a dress?"

"No." I was insulted. "I will not be bought."

"It's a great party."

"I'm not here to party."

"Brooklyn seems like she's here to party. And we can't break them up if we're not with them."

I opened my mouth to shoot down the idea, but I realized he was making sense.

If I couldn't get Brooklyn to skip the dance—which seemed like a tall order, given her level of excitement—maybe the next best thing was to follow her there. It would be a whole lot harder for her to avoid me if we were in the same room.

"Fine," I said to Max.

"You'll take the dress?"

"I'll go to the dance."

"Then you will need a dress."

"Layla?" Brooklyn asked, clearly puzzled by my silence.

"I'm here," I answered her.

Brooklyn sounded fragile now, vulnerable as she spoke. "I really, really love the dress."

"Fine," I said. "I'll come and see the dress."

Max spoke up. "Colton's suite is next to mine."

Max's words gave me pause on a whole bunch of fronts.

I'd made passionate love with Max right next door to where Brooklyn was staying? We could have been caught that very night. They might have seen us on the patio, or out in the hallway, or—or...

The elevator doors slid open. We'd arrived at the lobby.

"I'll be there in three minutes," I said.

"I can't wait to show you." Brooklyn ended the call.

"How do you want to play this?" Max asked as we made our way through the main lobby.

"Good afternoon, Mr. Kendrick," a staff member greeted him in passing.

"Afternoon, Brian," Max responded.

I couldn't help but comment. "Of course, you know him, too."

"He's the events manager."

Other staff members watched our progress. I realized they were wondering who I was.

"Just another date, people," I muttered under my breath. "He does this all the time."

"Pardon me?" Max asked.

"Everyone's staring at me."

"They're staring at me. They're wondering when I'm going to give them their next raise. So do we just up and admit we're going to the Twenties Tangle together? Or do you want me to casually bring it up? I can hang back and arrive after you, or we can tell them about the balloon trip."

"You mean the balloon crash."

"I wouldn't lead with that. It'll probably upset Brooklyn."

I knew there was wisdom in his advice.

"I'll go in first," I said. "You arrive casually in a few minutes and then mention you have an extra ticket—at an appropriate point."

"And the balloon adventure?"

"We'll play it by ear." It wasn't a secret, but if Brooklyn knew Max and I had spent virtually the entire day together, she'd start getting more ideas about us. I didn't need that, and neither did Max.

* * *

"If I don't buy you a dress, Colton will," Max said as we left Colton's suite. It was a mirror of Max's next door.

Brooklyn was thrilled when I'd agreed to come to the dance. I'd made them work to get my yes, and Max had played along quite brilliantly.

I figured Brooklyn would get all speculative on my feelings toward Max if I gave in too easily. Plus, I'd honestly held out hope that she'd change her mind and would spend the evening alone with me instead of going with Colton—wrong about that.

"You might as well pick it out for yourself," Max said.

I knew I didn't want to be indebted to Colton for a dress. And I knew Brooklyn would show up with something for me if she thought I had nothing to wear.

I decided Max was the lesser of two evils.

The other option was buying my own dress. A strong independent modern woman would likely insist on that.

But this strong independent modern woman had mortgage and car payments coming due, and she'd covered a whole lot of incidental expenses leading up to a wedding that might not even happen. Plus, I rationalized, it was Max's and Colton's fault I was in this mess, and this was no more than pocket change for Max.

I didn't really buy into that rationalization. But I did allow myself to be swayed by the mortgage payment and the fact that I'd only wear the dress once.

"Fine," I said to Max. "Buy me a stupid dress."

"You had to think a long time on that."

"I'm not thrilled about the idea of having a strange man buy me a dress."

"But…" he said.

"But what?"

"There has to be a *but*, since you said yes, anyway."

"But I have a mortgage payment coming up." I was going with blunt honesty from here on in. I didn't particularly care how embarrassing it got.

There was no point in pretending I had money. I was an ordinary schoolteacher with a nine-hundred-square-foot condo and a ten-year-old car.

He gave a low whistle. "Exactly how much are you planning to spend on this dress?"

I knew he was joking. At least I was pretty sure he was joking.

"A lot," I said. "I'm attending this dance under protest, and I have zero scruples about maxing out your credit card to look good doing it."

He grinned. "This I have got to see."

Before I knew it, we were out front of the hotel.

Max held up a hand, and a black SUV eased to a stop in front of us.

The driver jumped out, but Max was already opening the back door for me.

"Where to?" The driver asked.

"Crystal's."

"Yes, sir."

"Do they sell costumes?" I asked as I slid into the seat.

"They sell everything."

Max sat down beside me and the vehicle glided onto the Strip.

I watched the people on the crowded sidewalks while Max sent a text to someone.

I sent my own text, alerting Brooklyn to my dress-shopping expedition so she didn't get any strange ideas of her own.

A few blocks later we pulled up to a bank of glass doors set in a gleaming geometric building.

A man in a suit jacket opened Max's door.

"Mr. Kendrick," the man said. "I'm Dalton Leonard, an assistant manager here at the Crystal Shops."

"Hello, Dalton."

Max stood, then he turned to offer me his hand.

Feeling like I'd wandered into a fairy tale, I took his hand to steady myself.

"We're attending the Twenties Tangle," Max said.

Dalton turned his attention to me. "I'm happy to be of assistance, ma'am."

"Layla," I said to him and offered my hand.

He shook. "Of course, ma'am. Might I suggest Andante's on the second floor?"

"Sure." I wasn't about to argue. I was along for the ride on this one.

He gave a sharp nod. "Their selection of period dresses is wonderful. They also have modern ensembles with a nod to the past, if you'd like to go that route."

I wasn't at all sure what route I wanted to go.

"This way." Dalton gestured to the glass doors.

As we entered the opulent shopping mall, I was even less sure of what route I wanted to go—maybe straight back out the front door. I knew I'd joked about spending Max's money, but now that the reality of high-end Vegas shopping was staring me in the face, I didn't know if I had the nerve.

Don't get me wrong, I like designer brands. Brooklyn and I spent many happy hours haunting the outlet stores looking for good bargains. Brooklyn had a flair, and I had learned quite a lot over the years.

But paying full-blown retail in a place as fancy as this was enough to make my mouth go dry and double my pulse rate.

"You asked for it," Max whispered in my ear as we walked.

It was then that I realized I was still holding his hand.

"Are you testing me?"

"Maybe. If you want to back out, there's a used clothing store north off the Strip."

"There is?" I stopped.

I wished he'd said something sooner. I could afford to buy my own dress at a used clothing store. It was a perfect solution. Where else did a strong, independent, modern, *smart* woman go to buy a dress she'd only wear once?

Max tugged on my arm. "Oh, no you don't. We have a deal."

I peered at his smug expression. "You were testing me there, too, weren't you? There is no used clothing store."

"Not in your future. Dalton's getting away."

"Let him."

"That would be rude." Max kept tugging, and I started walking.

"I don't need a brand-new dress," I said.

"You may not need one, but you're getting one."

"I'll take the used option, thank you."

"That's way too much trouble, and not nearly as much fun."

I wasn't sure I was capable of having fun at this. It wasn't like I was going to enjoy the dance. This extravagant shopping trip was wasted on me, and Max should be spending his money on some other woman.

Wait a minute.

"Who were you planning on taking to the dance?" I asked.

"Nobody."

"You're lying."

"I'm not lying."

"The dance is tonight. You already had tickets. You

must have had a date. Is that who you texted in the car? Please don't tell me you broke some poor girl's heart."

"I didn't break anyone's heart. I texted the Crystal Shops office to have someone meet us out front so we didn't have to traipse all over the mall to find the right store. But thanks for the vote of confidence."

"What vote of confidence?"

"That I had the power to break a heart by breaking a date."

"Well…" I didn't exactly know what to say to that. I could deny it was what I meant. But I had absolutely no doubt he could break a woman's heart by breaking a date.

"It's a charity thing," he said. "I always buy tickets, even if I'm not in town. I wasn't planning to go."

Now I felt guilty instead of stupid. "I'm sorry I'm making you go."

"I offered. Here we are."

Dalton had stopped outside the doorway to a clothing store.

I could tell by the plush carpet, the gleaming racks and the wide distances between the displays that the prices were going to be sky-high.

"If this doesn't work for you," Dalton said, "try Silver's across the way." He pointed to a dazzling sign. "Or one floor directly up is Ace and Night. They also carry period clothing."

"Thank you, Dalton," Max said.

"Nancy Roth is the store manager here at Andante's. She'll be happy to help if you have questions. Or call me if I can be of any additional help." Dalton handed Max a business card, nodding to both of us before he walked away.

"You live in a weird world," I said to Max.

"It's the same world you live in."

"Not really."

He put a hand lightly on my back and ushered me into the store.

The gesture should have annoyed me, but it didn't. Strong, independent, modern me had been left somewhere back on the sidewalk. Fairy-tale princess me was about to buy a dress for the ball.

A clerk immediately stepped up to offer help, and in no time I had six dresses hanging inside my large dressing room.

One was opulent, with gold lamé fabric and black beading. It all but screamed expensive. I tried on a pink one instead and decided it wasn't my color. Then I tried one in a longer length, a pretty dove-gray tulle with a bow on the hip. I thought it made me look old.

"Are you coming out anytime soon?" Max called through the curtain.

"I don't love anything yet," I answered back.

"What about the blue?"

I took the blue dress from the hanger and slipped it over my head. It was satin on the sides with a long dark blue fringe at the midthigh hem, with nude fabric across the front covered in shimmering gold lace.

I'm not a prude by any means, but it made me look like a risqué pop-music star.

Still, I pulled open the curtain and stepped outside.

Max's jaw dropped. He didn't say a word, but his expression was comical.

"Maybe with the right shoes," I said.

"Definitely not in public."

"I'm not sure where exactly a person could wear this." Maybe in a stage show.

"My hotel suite," Max said under his breath.

I didn't think he meant for me to hear it. I pretended I

hadn't, but my skin heated at the image his words brought to mind.

I felt sexy as he stared at me, and my mind wandered back to our lovemaking.

His blue gaze hung on to mine until I shook myself free.

"Next," I said and turned back to the changing room.

The final dress was a simple white sheath with jeweled spaghetti straps and traditional white-tassel fringe layers along its length. The final strands of tassel ended above my knee.

It didn't look like much on the hanger, but it was a perfect fit. It came with a matching jeweled headband, and my auburn hair set off the white.

It didn't strike me as the most expensive of the choices, and that made me happy. Despite my threat to spend Max's money, I wasn't at all comfortable being extravagant. Though, judging by the store, nothing was going to be a bargain.

"Are you coming out?" he called.

I opened the curtain.

Max stared at me for a minute.

"Do you like it?" he asked.

"I do." I gave a turn so that he could see it from the back.

"You have good taste," he said.

I wasn't sure of his meaning. "I hope that doesn't mean it's expensive."

"It means it looks good."

The salesclerk reappeared. "Oh, that looks wonderful." Her tone was overly enthusiastic, which is what she got paid for. "I have just the right shoes," she said.

"Shoes?"

"You'll need shoes," Max said.

I knew that neither my boots nor my pool sandals were

going to do it. But I didn't want Max buying me shoes on top of everything else.

"Don't even think about protesting," Max said. "The outfit comes with accessories. Got a purse?"

"I don't—"

"Purse," Max called out to the clerk, who was making her way across the store.

She gave him a wave to show she'd heard.

"This is ridiculous," I said.

"This is pretty fun," Max said.

"I don't see how it's fun for you." I moved to use a three-way mirror.

"You'd be surprised."

The clerk returned with a pair of silver high-heel T-strap shoes with teardrop cutouts. She brought three white-and-silver purses in various styles.

I took the chair next to Max and tried on the shoes. They fit.

"This one," Max said, holding up a small white pleated satin clutch with jeweled silver handles.

"Your boyfriend has good taste," the clerk quietly said to me.

It was a sure bet that coming from the clerk on commission, "good taste" meant expensive. But Max looked intent on buying the purse.

"He's not my boyfriend," I said back in the same undertone. "This isn't my life."

Her expression turned conspiratorial—one member of the sisterhood to another. "You should try to change that."

Max came to his feet. "It looks like we've got ourselves an outfit. Unless you need earrings?"

"I don't need earrings," I quickly said.

"Don't be too hasty," the clerk said.

She might have been supporting the sisterhood, or she

could have been thinking about her own commission. Either way, I was standing firm.

Even a fairy-tale princess had to draw the line somewhere.

"No earrings."

Eight

"**Y**our dress is gorgeous." Brooklyn took in my outfit, reaching out to strum her fingers through the fringe across my stomach.

She looked stunning in a fitted, lacy midnight blue, gold-trimmed dress with a fringe brushing her thighs. She wore jewel earrings and a matching necklace that sparkled with both clear and blue stones.

"Tell me those aren't real," I said.

She touched one of the earrings. "I didn't ask."

"How could you not ask?"

"I didn't want to know."

"Brooklyn." I was shocked by her attitude. "How can you accept—" I couldn't help myself. I reached out to touch the stones on the necklace. I was willing to bet a whole lot that they were real. "*This* from another man."

"Colton isn't another man." She got a determined look on her face. "Layla, I have to tell James."

Panic welled up inside me. "You can't."

"I know I promised I'd think about it. But this isn't fair to either of them. It's not right."

"You can't know yet," I said. "You can't be completely sure."

Her tone and expression were firm and a little angry. "I'm completely sure."

Colton appeared, and I glared at him.

He did a double take of my expression, but then looked to Brooklyn. "Dance?"

"I have to go to the ladies' room," she said.

"I'll come—"

"Don't," she said with her own glare at me.

I rocked back from her sharp tone.

And then she was gone, and I was standing there facing Colton.

"She's terrified of hurting you," Colton said.

I felt my hackles rise. I didn't need this stranger telling me about Brooklyn's emotional state. I knew Brooklyn's emotional state. I always knew her emotional state.

Right now her emotional state was terrifying me.

"We've been best friends our whole lives," I said to Colton.

"She told me. She loves you a lot."

"Why are you doing this?" I asked him.

"I offered to walk away," he said.

I found it impossible to believe that. "Sure you did."

"Did you?" a third voice asked.

I looked up to find Max beside me.

Colton shifted his attention to his brother.

"More than once," he said.

"Maybe you should insist," Max said.

I hadn't really expected Max to back me up when push came to shove. I felt good that he was on my side. I felt less alone in the fight.

"If I thought it was best for her, I would," Colton said.

"It is best for her," I said. I believed that with every fiber of my being.

"Are you going to marry her?" Max asked.

Colton's tone was incredulous. "We've known each other for four days."

"That's my point. You're taking away her happily-ever-after to offer what? A fling?"

"Don't insult Brooklyn. This is not a fling."

Max shifted a little closer to his brother. "What is it?"

"It's two people discovering each other and realizing they might not be able to live apart."

"That's ridiculous," I said.

It wasn't my most eloquent argument, but it had the advantage of being true.

"You're not being fair to her," Max said.

Brooklyn reappeared in time to hear Max's words. "You know nothing about me," she told him tartly. To Colton she asked, "Can we please dance?"

"Yes, we can." Colton took her arm.

"Don't call James," I called out to Brooklyn.

"I'm going to dance," she replied, walking away.

"What do I do?" I asked myself as much as Max.

The image of James getting a breakup call from Brooklyn was too much to bear. I thought about rushing home so I would be there when it happened. But there was nothing I could say or do to soften the blow.

"They seem really sure," Max said.

"You're giving up already?"

"Not if you don't want me to."

"I don't want you to."

Max nodded. "Okay. I'll talk to Colton."

"Thank you."

"In the meantime." He glanced around the big ballroom. "We might as well dance."

I didn't much feel like dancing. Then again, I didn't much feel like standing here worrying, either.

"You look beautiful," Max said.

The soft glow of his gaze made me warm.

I felt beautiful. I felt guilty for feeling beautiful, but there it was.

I was at an amazing event, in a really fun outfit, with a superhot guy. And there was nothing I could do this exact moment to help either James or Brooklyn.

I knew enough to know that particular rationalization was true. But I couldn't decide if I was being logical or self-centered.

I was probably both. But it didn't change any of the facts.

"You look great yourself," I told him.

He looked genuinely pleased by the compliment, even though he had to already know he was the best-looking guy in a very crowded room.

It occurred to me then that he must always be the best-looking guy in the room. There wasn't much competition for him anywhere on the planet. Maybe Colton. But when you took in the subtleties, Max easily beat Colton.

"Let's dance," I said, and I linked my arm with his.

"Now you're talking."

The band was playing a slow song, and I nestled into Max's arms. It felt good to give in and accept that I'd done my best. I was tired now, and I had to take a breather.

My world shrank to Max, the warmth of his skin, the movement of his body and the beat of his heart.

He was a better dancer than I'd expected. He was tall, and he was sturdy and muscular. I was surprised he was also graceful.

"You're good at this," I said, gliding along, happy to follow where he led.

"You're very easy to dance with."

"It's more than just that. You've practiced, or maybe

had lessons." I tipped my head to look up at him. "Did you take dance lessons?"

"Guilty. My parents insisted."

"Why? I mean, of all things, why would they insist you learn to dance." I indulged myself in tracing the contours of his bicep and shoulder. "You're not exactly built to do it professionally."

"My grandparents thought socializing was important for the business. Colton and I were constantly conscripted to entertain teenage girls."

"Boo-hoo. That must have been such a hardship."

"Most of them were a foot taller than us."

"Late bloomers?"

"A little bit."

"I find that hard to imagine." I couldn't picture Max as a short teenager.

"I was skinny, too," he said with a laugh.

"I thought you played second base."

"Not in junior high. What about you?"

"Skinny, yes. And I had braces. Plus with the red hair and freckles."

He smoothed a hand over my hair. His touch sent a warmth flowing down my spine.

"I like this color," he said.

"I like it now, too, but I sure didn't like it in high school."

"And I like your freckles," he said on a smile. "They're subtle, but interesting...pretty."

"They faded a lot."

"Well, you're perfect now."

I couldn't help a short chuckle at that. "You're the one who's perfect. I expect the girls couldn't get enough of you after you made it through puberty."

"Volume has never been a problem."

"A little full of ourselves, are we?"

"That's not the way I meant it. It's easy enough to get a date. The hard part is finding someone you want to spend more than an evening with."

"You must have had girlfriends."

"A few."

"When was the last one?"

"I'm not going to talk to you about my girlfriends."

"Come on. Dish."

"You tell me about your boyfriends."

"All imperfect. Every one of them had a fatal flaw." I was only half joking. "It turns out I'm very fussy."

"Yeah? How am I stacking up so far?"

I couldn't read his voice, so I looked up to see his expression. I couldn't read that, either.

"You're not my boyfriend."

"Not yet."

Now I knew he had to be joking.

"I'm gone tomorrow, next day at the latest," I reminded him.

I was reminded of Brooklyn, and that brought a wave of worry and sadness.

Max seemed to sense my mood, and he drew me closer.

"You really are going to have to give her space."

I knew it was my only choice. Brooklyn was angry with me right now. Anything I said was going to make it worse.

I pushed her from my mind.

Instead, I marveled at how perfectly I fit in Max's arms. I mean every curve, every nook, everything about me matched perfectly with him. I'd never felt such a huge, encompassing, incredible hug in all of my life.

I didn't want to move. I just wanted to stand here molded against him while I absorbed his essence.

I remembered being naked in his arms. I closed my

eyes and inhaled his scent, taking myself back to those few hours in his hotel suite. Arousal pulsed through me, tickling my skin, heating my core. I wanted him all over again.

He kissed my neck, his hot tender lips sprinkling shivers of delight from the curve of my shoulder to the tip of my breasts.

I barely stopped myself from moaning out loud.

I wanted his kiss. I wanted his mouth. I wanted the deep soul-satisfying kisses that had guided me to paradise.

"Kiss me," I whispered.

"Yes, ma'am."

His lips unerringly found mine. They touched lightly at first, then firmer, then harder.

I squeezed my arms around his neck, and he pressed the small of my back, arching me against his hard thighs.

His tongue thrust into my mouth and I answered with enthusiasm. I knew where this was leading, and I couldn't wait to get there. Max was a fantastic lover. I wanted nothing more than to stop time and be swallowed all over again by his spell.

A warning ticked at my brain. I ignored it, but it became insistent.

Something was wrong. I was missing some vital piece of information.

The music swelled, and I remembered we were in a ballroom. We were in public, surrounded by other people.

My eyes flew open with my gasp.

"What?" he asked.

I looked frantically around us to see who might be watching. But Max had danced us into a dark corner. No one could see us. I didn't need to worry.

My fear disappeared. But Max still held me, so my arousal was strong as ever. I throbbed where we touched.

My lips tingled from his kisses. I wanted everything we'd had that night—all over again.

Our gazes locked. Heat seemed to leap through the space between us.

It was odd the way it happened, like we had some kind of cosmic connection. Make that a solar connection, or microwaves or something. It was hot and magnetic and irresistible.

"Layla." His voice was strained.

"Can we go back?" I asked. My voice sounded breathless, like an Old Hollywood movie star posing provocatively in a long silhouette dress.

"You mean to the hotel?" he asked.

"Yes." That was exactly what I meant. "Your room. Now."

"Oh, yeah." He was moving for the exit before the words were out of his mouth.

There was a privacy screen in the limo, and I could only hope the intercom was turned off because Max pulled me straight into his lap. I willingly picked up the kisses right where we'd left off.

His jacket was stiff and boxy, so I reached underneath. I felt my way up his chest, over his pecs.

I felt his heartbeat. It was deep, strong and fast.

My heart was racing, too, pumping energy, sending hormonal messages to every corner of my body. I loved the feel of arousal, the heightened senses, the tingling waves of heat that left my body begging to be touched.

I found Max's hand. I set it on my bare thigh.

His touch was hot and sure.

He slipped his palm higher, which was what I wanted. It was exactly what I wanted.

I arched and moaned into our kiss. I teased his tongue

with mine, clinging to his broad shoulders, shamelessly enjoying the stokes of his fingertips going higher and higher.

When he pushed aside my panties, I knew I should stop him. I was willingly playing with fire, and we were in the back of a limo. It wasn't public, but it wasn't the privacy of a hotel room, either.

It wouldn't take more than a word or a movement to call a halt, to put this on hold until we were safely locked in his hotel suite.

In a minute, I told myself. Just one minute more.

But his touch grew more intimate, and I gripped his shoulders. Tension spiraled tighter and tighter within me. My brain started to hum, and a deep pulse grew to life.

I started to gasp, and my hips took on a life of their own pushing against Max's hand. I was past stopping, past slowing down. It was going to happen, and it was going to happen right now.

I bit my lip to keep quiet, but I moaned just the same.

I buried my face in the crook of Max's shoulder and shuddered as waves of pleasure crested over and over.

They finally slowed, then stopped, and I tried to catch my breath. "I'm..." I didn't exactly know what to say.

"Don't you dare feel bad about that," Max said in a low rumble.

I could feel his voice in his chest.

"And don't you dare feel embarrassed." He drew a deep breath himself. "You are amazing."

The limo slowed.

Max extracted his hand and smoothed down my dress as the limo came to a stop.

"Amazing," he repeated and gave me a tender kiss.

"How do I look?" I asked, aware that we were about to step into the bright lights of the portcullis and the lobby.

"Perfect," he said with a smile.

"You know what I mean."

"A little flushed. A little bright-eyed. It makes you even more beautiful."

The compliment made me happy. It was silly. I mean, what else was he going to say in a moment like this? Still, I liked it.

The driver opened the door.

"Ready?" Max asked me.

"I guess." It wasn't like I could get more ready by sitting here.

He stepped out first, then held his hand for me. He kept my hand in his as we walked to the door.

It was beginning to feel very natural, holding Max's hand while we walked.

Somewhere deep in my brain I knew that feeling was dangerous. But I wasn't using the rational parts of my brain, not right now, not tonight. Tonight I was letting emotion take over completely. Everything I had to analyze, rationalize and worry about would still be there tomorrow.

"Good evening, Mr. Kendrick," the doorman said.

"Good evening, Carlos."

"It still amazes me how you do that," I said to Max as we walked on.

"Practice," he said.

We turned toward his suite, silent as we made our way down the corridor.

He flashed the lock with his key card, and we were inside the darkened room.

"You need anything?" he asked me as the door swung shut.

"Do you?" I asked, turning to face him.

"Nothing but you."

"Same."

I was back in his arms. His kisses were more frantic this time. I could understand that. He was running behind me in the lovemaking, and I was feeling pretty frantic myself.

With one hand, he stripped off his jacket and shirt.

Then he pulled my dress up over my head. He jerked off my panties. I thought they might have torn, but I couldn't have cared less.

I pushed off his pants. A condom came from somewhere. And then he was lifting me, bracing me against the wall, kissing me deeper than ever and pushing inside me.

"Yes-s-s," I hissed, happily surprised by the strength of my arousal returning so quickly.

Usually the second time was milder for me, a muted echo of the first round. But not tonight. Tonight I simply couldn't get enough of Max.

His pace was firm and steady. His hands cradled my thighs. With every stroke, he brushed the tips of my sensitized breasts.

My every nerve ending was squealing with pleasure. My core was pulling tighter and tighter. I had to remind myself to breathe.

"Layla," Max called out on a gasp.

"Yes," I responded. "Oh, yes."

When I thought it couldn't get any better, it did. The earth paused and the room spun around me.

His pace increased, and he pressed me hard, dead center, and I cried out as pleasure cascaded higher and longer and deeper than ever before.

We pulsed together, slick and sliding, our chests pressing together as we dragged in deep breaths.

Max wrapped me tight. He kissed my neck, then my shoulder, then my lips.

"You look pretty content," he whispered.

It took me a second to form any words. "Actually, I'm pretty great."

He chuckled low. "I'm so glad to hear that. And I agree. You're pretty great."

I smiled. "Right back at you."

He kissed me again.

"Thirsty?" he asked. "Hungry?"

"I don't know what I am." I'd never felt quite this disembodied before.

I mean, I'd had sex in the past, with boyfriends I liked a lot. And they weren't bad at it. They were fine at it. But this was different. I couldn't put my finger on why or how, but it was a completely different experience with Max.

"Well, I've worked up an appetite," he said.

He slowly lowered me to the floor. "I can order something while we shower. Any preferences?"

"Something excessive," I said. "Something decadent and delicious, completely without redeeming qualities."

"Decadent and delicious coming up," he said. "Meet me in the shower?"

I woke up in Max's bed, in Max's arms.

It felt right. And that was worrisome—though it wasn't worrisome enough for me to move.

Okay, maybe it was worrisome enough for me to move.

I glanced at the bedside clock and discovered it was almost nine. Now that was enough to get me moving. My stolen night was over, and I needed to get back to Brooklyn.

I shifted the covers and moved my legs.

Max's arm snaked around me. "Don't go."

"I have to go."

"Why?"

"I need to find Brooklyn."

He heaved an exaggerated sigh. "Story of your life. Okay. I'm up." He sat up in the bed.

"You don't have to get up with me."

"I promised I'd help."

"That's true. You did." It wasn't something I intended to hold him to this morning.

I don't know why last night had changed that. But it had.

I wrapped myself in a plush robe and headed for the bathroom. There I washed my face and combed out my hair.

I often went without makeup, but I had to admit, I wasn't looking forward to taking the elevator back to my room in the flapper dress. Given how many people had attended the event last night, it was going to be pretty obvious that I'd made a last-minute decision to sleep in someone else's room—not my best look.

I made my way from the bathroom into the living room of the suite.

Max was pouring coffee from a room-service cart.

He turned and held out a cup for me. "Cream and sugar, right?"

"You just get better and better," I said, accepting the cup.

"I got you something else," he said.

"A blueberry bagel?" I asked hopefully.

We'd snacked on fancy pastries and liquor-laced hot chocolate last night. I knew the hotel bakery was out of this world.

"We can get those, too." He pointed to a shopping bag on the sofa.

I checked it to find a pair of black yoga pants and an oversize T-shirt. Beneath them were a pair of flat sandals.

"I figured you'd be overdressed for the lobby this morning."

"That was very thoughtful."

He gave a shrug. "You want me to order you a bagel?"

"I don't have time."

I took my coffee and the new clothes into the bedroom.

Max followed, then leaned against the doorjamb and watched me change.

"What are your plans?" he asked.

I stepped into the butter-soft yoga pants. "I'm going to stop in my room and then find Brooklyn."

"What do you want me to do?"

"Keep Colton occupied while I talk to her?"

I was thinking about tactics. I couldn't be confrontational anymore. It simply wasn't going to work. I supposed I could beg, but I didn't see that as a long-term strategy. I thought I might let her talk it through. Maybe when she heard it out loud she'd see the flaws in her judgment.

"I can do that," Max said.

"While you're at it…" I wasn't sure how far I should press him.

He didn't owe me anything. And I didn't want it to seem like I had expectations after the night we spent together.

"I could help him see the error of his ways?" Max asked.

I paused before pulling the T-shirt over my head. "I don't want you to think I expect that."

"You demanded it yesterday."

"Yesterday was yesterday."

He sauntered close to me. "Last night was one for the record books. But it doesn't change a thing between us."

"Okay," I agreed, liking yet not liking the sentiment.

"I'll still help you any way I can."

"I appreciate that."

"You go find Brooklyn. I'll make sure my brother has his head on straight."

I stuffed my feet into the sandals, took a final drink of the coffee and headed for the door.

Max took hold of my arm as I passed, stopping me, and pulled me in for a tender kiss.

"Bye," he whispered.

"Bye," I whispered back.

We both smiled, and I knew I had to get myself out of there quick.

Getting the elevator to my floor meant a trip back through the lobby.

As I wound my way through the morning crowd, I was enormously grateful for the change of clothes.

Max was a nice guy.

He was a great guy.

I felt light remembering our lovemaking, floating even, focusing on his smile, his laugh, our shower and the decadent pastries.

"Layla?" James's voice stopped me cold. "I tried your room," he continued from behind me. "But neither of you answered."

I turned. I had no choice. James was here. He was here in Vegas, and everything was about to fall apart.

"Where were you?" he asked.

"At breakfast," I said.

The coffee in Max's room didn't exactly qualify as breakfast, but short of lying to James's face it was the best I could do on such short notice.

"Why didn't you answer your phone?" he persisted.

"Battery." That part was true. It was low last night at the dance. But I had to turn the tables on the conversation before his questions got impossible. "Why are you here? I thought you said you'd wait?"

It was obvious he was annoyed. "I've waited long enough. I know you don't want Brooklyn to marry me."

His words rang nonsensically through my brain. "What?"

"You've been jealous—"

"Back up. *What?*"

"Of me and Brooklyn."

"Jealous of you and *Brooklyn*?" The idea was preposterous.

"You know it's true."

"It is absolutely not true." It couldn't be further from what was going on here.

"You've been that way all along," James said, looking more disgusted than I'd ever seen him.

He, too, had lost every ounce of reason. First Brooklyn and now James. Everyone around me was going absolutely batty.

"You're not making any sense at all," I said.

He shifted closer to me. His tone was laced with annoyance and accusation. "You know exactly what I'm talking about."

I stared him down. "I really don't."

I might not be perfect, but I sure wasn't envious. I'd been fighting tooth and nail here for James. I wasn't his rival. I was darn well his best friend!

James gave a flat chuckle. "The Fuzzy Lake trips. The club membership. Last Christmas. I tried to tell myself you'd get over it. I thought once we actually got married, you'd back off and give us some space. But *this*—" he gestured around the hotel lobby "—*this* nonsense is off-the-charts."

I stared at my brother in silence. I had nothing. I truly had nothing here.

"She's marrying *me*," he barked. "Not you. And this

best-friend-and-intimate-companion-at-the-expense-of-everyone-else thing has got to stop, *now*."

I stepped backward from his growing anger.

A band was tightening around my chest. I wanted to fight back, but I told myself to calm down. Shouting at James wasn't going to change his mind.

I pretended I was in class, that I was confronting an unreasonable teenager. I dredged up a calm voice. "James, I don't want to come between you and Brooklyn."

He coughed out another laugh of disbelief. "Right."

"Seriously, James."

"Seriously, Layla."

We both stared at each other.

"I've been watching it for years," he said.

"Then you've been delusional for years."

I could never have guessed he felt this way. I thought he liked that me and Brooklyn were close. We were like sisters, better even, we were perfect sisters. There wasn't a reason in the world to be jealous of me.

"I don't think so," he said.

I moved in. "James, you are wrong."

He clamped his jaw. But I could see in his eyes that he was thinking.

"If I'm wrong," he finally said, "then prove it. Give her back."

"I haven't—"

He talked right over top of me. "Quit monopolizing Brooklyn's time. End this stupid trip so she can come home."

"I'm not—"

My breath stalled.

There was Brooklyn.

She was walking across the lobby with Colton. Arm

in arm, they were talking and laughing. They looked for all the world like a couple in love.

"Not what?" James's annoyed voice sounded a long way off.

My expression must have given me away because he turned to see where I was looking.

Brooklyn spotted him and stopped dead.

"Who is *that*?" James asked.

My brain flatlined for a moment. I was honestly incapable of having a thought, never mind making a sound.

But then inspiration hit me.

"That's Max," I blurted out.

I started for them, walking as fast as I dared to the frozen Brooklyn with Colton standing beside her.

I could hear James following me.

"Max," I called out as soon as we were in range. "I'm over here. You remember I talked about my brother, James? James, I told you I'd met someone here. This is Max Kendrick."

My voice was way too high, and I was talking way too fast. I could only hope James would chalk my near panicked tone up to our fight.

I pointedly linked my arm with Colton's, pulling him to me, putting a few more inches between him and Brooklyn.

"Were you just at the gym?" I asked Brooklyn, broadly hinting that should be her story.

"Max Kendrick," Colton interjected smoothly, distracting James by offering to shake his hand.

It worked.

"James Gillen, Brooklyn's fiancé." James shook Colton's hand.

It was the first time I'd ever liked Colton.

Brooklyn finally found her voice. "I didn't expect you to come," she said to James.

"I got tired of waiting. And, frankly, I'm about done with the two of you."

The blood drained from Brooklyn's face.

"James thinks I'm monopolizing you," I blurted out. There was an edge of annoyance in my tone. But then I was still pretty annoyed by that accusation.

James faced Brooklyn and took her hands in his. "You two have had your fun. I've tried to be patient. But we've got responsibilities. There are dozens of things to do this week for the wedding."

Brooklyn looked my way.

James gave me a glare that seemed to say Brooklyn was making his point about my relationship with her.

I ignored him. I actually had bigger problems. I had to figure out what Brooklyn was trying to convey.

Her look said she didn't want me to take the heat. My look told her to keep her big fat mouth shut. This was way too important to worry about me.

I'd talk to James later.

"Where's your ring?" James asked Brooklyn, frowning as he lifted her hands.

She looked at her fingers. "I…" The seconds ticked by, but I couldn't help her with this one.

She finally found her voice. "I took it off to go in the pool. It's a little loose. I've lost a bit of weight. You know, trying to make sure the wedding dress is perfect."

"I thought you were at the gym," James said.

"I'm going to the pool next."

James looked her up and down. It was obvious he felt like something wasn't right. "Where's your suit?"

"In our room," I quickly interjected. "She bought a new one. You're going to love it."

"Can we find somewhere to sit down?" James asked Brooklyn. Then he looked at me. "Alone?"

I knew that was what had to happen. And I knew that from here on in, it was up to James. This was his chance to tip the scales in his favor. I could only hope he didn't treat Brooklyn the way he'd treated me. If he did, the wedding would surely be canceled.

"We should get out of your way," I said to nobody in particular. But I gave a tug on Colton's arm, hoping he'd continue with my ruse.

And then I spotted Max.

He grinned as he sped up and strode toward us.

Then he frowned when he saw me on Colton's arm, confusion coming over his expression.

My heart was beating hard against my chest. If James turned around and saw Max…

Max slowed his steps, taking in all four of us.

His eyes widened ever so slightly, and I caught the moment where he figured out what was going on. He veered off into a women's clothing shop.

I nearly sagged with relief.

"Brooklyn?" James prompted.

"There's a lounge over there," I said and pointed in the opposite direction of the clothing shop. "It should be quiet this time of day."

I gave Brooklyn a quick hug. "Don't say a thing," I whispered in her ear. "We'll talk later."

"Tell—" she began.

"Shhh!" I cautioned.

She swallowed and gave me a slight nod.

"Can we hit the pool?" I asked Colton.

"Love to," he told me. He switched his gaze from Brooklyn to me and mustered up a smile. "Let's go buy you that new suit first." His nod to the clothing store told me he'd seen Max, just like I had.

"Perfect," I said. "See you two later."

I hated to leave Brooklyn on her own with James, but I had to get Colton out of there, and I had to trade him in for Max before things got any worse.

We found Max quickly.

"What happened?" he asked.

"James is here," I said.

"I got that," Max said. "Does he know anything?"

"No so far." So far, I was the bad guy. I was still miffed about that. More than miffed, really—talk about coming right out of the blue.

"What are you going to do?" Max asked Colton.

Colton glanced back over his shoulder, but Brooklyn and James had disappeared around the corner.

"This is more about what Brooklyn's going to do," Colton said.

"I told him you were Colton," I said to Max. Then I thought about the phraseology for a second. "Or that Colton was you. You know what I mean. I didn't know how else to explain him."

"Is Brooklyn going to tell him the truth?" Max asked.

"No," I said.

"Maybe," Colton said.

"No," I repeated. "Not yet. I told her to keep quiet for now."

"Of course you did," Colton said.

"She's not ready," I told him, hoping it was true.

"It has to be on her own time," Max said.

Colton looked like he wanted to argue. But then the fight seemed to go out of him. "In that case, Layla, we should get her stuff into your room."

I had to give him credit for a very good idea.

"There's only one bed in Layla's room," Max pointed out.

"We'll tell James there was a sale." I knew he wouldn't

be overly shocked that Brooklyn and I would share a king-size bed. We'd done it before.

"You better slip her a key," Max said to me.

"I can do that."

"And then..." Max said.

"And then," Colton said with a sigh of resignation, "we wait. It's up to her."

"You bet it's up to her," I said.

"Layla." Colton sounded like he was summoning patience. "I want what's best for Brooklyn."

"No, *I* want what's best for Brooklyn," I countered.

Colton shook his head. "Difference is, I want Brooklyn to be happy. You want James to be happy."

"That's not fair."

Colton's feelings for Brooklyn couldn't hold a candle to mine.

For a second, my reaction gave me pause. I was forced to wonder about James's tirade. Was there a grain of truth in his accusations? Was it possible I'd hampered their relationship all this time?

Was it my fault she wasn't sure of her feelings?

"I love her," Colton said.

"You barely know her," I said.

"This isn't getting us anywhere," Max interjected.

Max was right, but I couldn't back off, especially if I was partly to blame.

"What happens in a year?" I asked Colton. "Or a month? Or a week? What happens when you lose interest in her?"

"That's not going to happen."

"It's impossible for you to know what's going to happen. Brooklyn isn't the woman you've met here. She's on vacation. She's going through a thing. The real Brooklyn is completely different. She has foibles. She has flaws."

"She squeezes the toothpaste in the middle?" Colton asked with sarcasm.

"She's addicted to pistachio nuts. She binge-watches fashion TV. She refuses to fill her car up with gas."

Both Colton and Max blinked at me as if I'd forgotten my own name.

"And a whole bunch of other things," I said. "Things that James knows about and accepts and loves."

"I'm not giving Brooklyn up," Colton said. "But if she wants to give me up, I'll step aside."

I didn't believe him.

"I'll step aside without a fight. In fact, I'll back off right now. I'll make myself scarce for the day or a couple days, whatever it takes." He started to nod. "She should spend some time with James. That's the only way she'll know for sure."

I agreed with him. What's more, the offer seemed too good to be true.

"Her engagement ring is in the safe in my room," Colton said. "Let's go get it, and move her things."

"You'd really do that?" I asked him.

I was primed to dislike him. I preferred not to like him. But even I had to admit this was an honorable thing to do.

"I'm doing it," he said.

Max gave me an I-told-you-so look.

I couldn't say I exactly blamed him. Colton was busy validating the arguments Max had been making all along—that Colton wasn't despicable.

He was still wrong for Brooklyn. But maybe, hopefully, he'd meet a nice woman in the future.

I could wish him well somewhere that was not with me and my friends and family. I could do that.

Nine

It was hours before I got Brooklyn alone.

We were at the Triple Palm Café in the hotel atrium and the sun was going down.

"How are you feeling?" I asked her, leaning in as James left the restaurant to talk to the front desk about a room.

He'd been terse with me since I'd joined them fifteen minutes ago. I knew he wanted me to leave them alone, but I couldn't stay completely away. There was way too much at risk.

Brooklyn's happy expression faded as James walked away. She looked completely miserable. "I'm more confused than ever."

I didn't know what to say to that. I didn't exactly know what she meant. I hoped it was a good thing. I hoped seeing James had reminded her of what they had together.

"Confused how?" I asked.

"James is…you know, he's James. He's sweet and patient, and he's always so good to me."

Sweet was debatable in my books after this morning. But I didn't disagree. I didn't want to interrupt her flow.

"I know what he wants, and I know where we're going, and I can still see our future together so clearly."

I nodded.

"But, Colton." She gave a sigh. "He's…"

I waited.

She seemed to be searching for the right word.

"New?" I prompted.

"Exciting, fun, exhilarating."

"He's got a lot of money to throw around," I said.

I still thought it was an uneven playing field tilted toward Colton.

Brooklyn looked like she was disappointed in me. Well, join the club. "You know it's not just that," she said.

"Can I ask…" I wasn't sure I was ready to take the plunge. But my gut told me it was all-or-nothing time.

Brooklyn waved a hand that said caution should go well and truly to the wind. "Ask away."

"Do you know how Colton feels about you? I mean do you really, honestly know? People aren't always what they seem."

I told myself I wasn't betraying Colton by questioning his motives and his morals. It was a legitimate question, a real concern. He trotted around the country, maybe around the globe for all I knew, romancing a huge variety of different women.

From what I'd seen of him online, he was active in city after city, at event after event. I'd counted no less than a dozen different women on his arm in the past couple of years. He didn't seem like the kind of guy who was in it for the long haul.

"I'm not looking for a guarantee from Colton," Brooklyn said.

"If it wasn't for Colton, would you be giving up on James?"

Brooklyn had to think about that one.

"Maybe," she said. "I don't know. Maybe not."

"So—at least in some ways—you're pinning your future on Colton."

"I'm not."

"Come on, Brooklyn. This is me."

"Okay, maybe I am, in some ways. I want to be with him. I really want to be with him."

"I'd so hate to see you make a mistake. After this first blush of lust—"

She looked genuinely insulted. "It's not lust."

"Okay. I'm sorry. Infatuation then. But after the first blush wears off, you could be left with nothing. You might spend the rest of your life regretting your choice. Can you tell me right here, right now, with one hundred percent certainty that you're positive you won't regret giving James up, giving up your life, your wonderful, incredible life together? Can you?"

Brooklyn sat back in her chair. "Nothing is one hundred percent."

"Lots of things are one hundred percent."

We both fell silent.

"What about tonight?" I asked.

"What about it?"

"James is getting a room."

Brooklyn didn't seem to comprehend.

"For the two of you," I said. "To sleep in. Together."

"We don't need to have sex."

I tried not to spend much time—any time at all, really— thinking about my brother's sex life. But this was a pretty obvious problem.

"You don't think he might expect it?" I asked.

Again, Brooklyn wasn't keeping up with the implications.

She looked at me blankly.

"You can't—" I realized my voice was getting loud and

I lowered it. "You can't jump from sleeping with Colton to sleeping with James like—" I snapped my fingers "—that. I mean, I don't mean to get all judgey or anything."

Brooklyn reared back. "I'm not sleeping with Colton."

I stilled. I mentally backtracked over the past few days. "What?"

"You thought I was sleeping with Colton?"

I didn't know what to say. I'd been sleeping with Max, and I'd just assumed that Brooklyn and Colton were also burning up the sheets.

"Thanks a ton," Brooklyn said.

"I'm sorry. I mean, you've clearly been…"

I wasn't exactly sure how to phrase it. They thought they were falling for each other, romantically obviously. And wouldn't that normally include sex?

Apparently not. My opinion of Colton went up another notch.

"I'm not cheating on James," Brooklyn said.

"I'm sorry," I repeated. There wasn't much more I could do but apologize.

"Would you cheat on your fiancé?" she asked.

"I've never had a fiancé."

"Well, you wouldn't. I know you wouldn't. And I wouldn't, either."

"I don't think I would."

For some reason I pictured Max. I knew there was no way in the world I'd ever cheat on Max, engaged or not.

Not that we'd ever be engaged. Not that we were even truly dating. But while I was sleeping with him, there's no way I'd have any interest whatsoever in another man.

I gave myself a moment to think that through.

"So you're deciding this without even sleeping with Colton?"

"There's no other way," Brooklyn said.

I almost asked her if she wanted to sleep with Colton, but then I realized that wouldn't do anything for James's side in this.

Brooklyn had to want to sleep with Colton. She had to be dying to sleep with Colton. That is, if she felt at all about Colton like I did about Max.

"You know James so much better," I said, instead.

"You're right."

I caught sight of James coming back down the path toward the café.

He had a glare for me that clearly said "Back off."

"Here he comes," I told Brooklyn.

She swallowed. "Can we order a drink?"

"Do you think it will help?"

"I don't think it will hurt."

"I better not stay," I said.

James pulled his chair back to sit down, his attention on Brooklyn to the exclusion of me. "These prices are outrageous."

"We're lucky we got a sale," I said, sticking with my story.

"There weren't any discounted rooms available today," he said, looking my way, then he looked irritated.

"Did you book something?" I asked, ignoring his attitude.

"Just for one night." He reached out and took Brooklyn's hand. "We need to go home tomorrow. Your mom's antsy about the dress and the cake, and there are still details to work out about the rehearsal dinner. I told them lobster and filet, but you need to look at the menu."

"Do they have the coconut-cream pie?" Brooklyn asked.

"I'm sure they'll make it available if that's what you

want. I had to confirm the violet arrangement for the centerpieces."

Brooklyn smiled. "That was my favorite."

He gave her a kiss on the hand. "I know it was your favorite. I want everything to be your favorite. And for that, you need to come home."

James slid his gaze to me. "Layla can always stay a couple of days on her own if it's that important to her."

"It's not Layla's fault," Brooklyn said.

"You don't need to defend her."

Brooklyn looked confused. "I'm only telling—"

"There's no reason for me to stay," I interrupted.

Brooklyn gazed into James's eyes.

After a moment, she looked down at their clasped hands. His were strong and wide. Hers sparkled with the diamond ring.

She tipped up her chin.

She squared her shoulders.

A bird swooped and chirped from the tree above us, joined by three of its friends.

I found myself holding my breath.

"Okay," Brooklyn said in a hollow voice. "We can catch a flight in the morning."

James had his phone out in an instant to book with the airline.

I was filled with relief.

But a split second later, I thought of Max, and my relief turned to disappointment. I told myself to buck up. I'd gotten exactly what I'd wanted, what I'd been fighting for, for days now.

My fling with Max might have been pretty great. It might have been fantastic. But it was always going to be temporary. It was always going to end exactly this way—

with me leaving and him moving on to the next hotel in the next city with the next woman.

Self-pity wasn't going to change a thing.

"Congratulations on your success," Max said. His tone was considerably less than sincere.

"I'm not going to apologize for being right," I told him.

After leaving Brooklyn and James, I'd come straight to Max's suite, finding Colton there, as well.

I hadn't wanted to say anything to Colton about Brooklyn's decision. But my expression must have tipped him off.

He guessed, and I couldn't lie.

"You're not right," Colton said to me. "And neither is Brooklyn." His voice was laced with a steely determination that made me nervous.

I knew he'd promised to let her decide. But right now he didn't look like a guy who was about to give up the fight.

"You said it was Brooklyn's call," I reminded him, putting an edge into my own tone.

"Is she at least going to talk to me?" he asked.

"I don't know." I didn't.

When I'd walked into Max's suite, I was operating on the assumption that Brooklyn would talk to Colton directly. But thinking it through now, I wasn't sure how that could happen with James by her side. And my brother didn't show any signs of leaving his fiancée's side before he got her on that plane tomorrow morning.

I was torn. Part of me couldn't help but sympathize with Colton. In his shoes, I'd sure want a final conversation with Brooklyn. On the other hand, judging by the expression on his face, if he got the chance he might try to change her mind.

I couldn't imagine how hard that would be on Brooklyn. I didn't even want to speculate about whether it might work. It was better for everyone if Colton didn't get the chance.

"James got them a room," I said.

Colton's jaw went hard. He swore.

Max shook his head, looking disappointed.

Colton marched for the door.

I didn't like where this was going. "You won't—"

He shot me a hard look, and I closed my mouth.

"Break my word?" he asked. "No, Layla. I'm not going to break my word. This is Brooklyn's decision. I can't force her to give me a real shot."

"She did," I felt forced to point out.

Colton stopped with his hand on the doorknob. "Not really. She went back to him before we had a chance."

Max touched my arm, and I knew he wanted me to stop talking. It was obvious he didn't want to upset Colton any more than necessary.

"She has a deadline," I said.

Colton sneered at my logic. "Weddings can be postponed."

"There are five hundred guests."

"It's the rest of her life."

The way he said it, something about his expression got me worrying.

I wasn't worried he'd break his word. Oh, no, I was worried that he was right. We were standing here talking about the rest of Brooklyn's life.

Letting my mind follow his logic for a minute, I tried to imagine canceling the wedding. I pictured my parents' reactions. My dad would freak out about the cost. My mom would focus on the social embarrassment.

Then I pictured Brooklyn's parents. They'd be baffled. I'd had several days to mull the idea, and I was baffled.

They thought James was the perfect man for Brooklyn. He was successful, professional, kind and smart, with two feet firmly planted on the ground.

They'd never forgive her for letting him get away.

Brooklyn's parents knew her well, just like I knew her well. If all of us, including Brooklyn, thought James was the right choice, he must be the right choice. Seeing James had obviously put everything in perspective and solidified her decision.

Colton wasn't even a fling. She hadn't even slept with him. How could they possibly understand their feelings for one another when their entire relationship had been platonic?

"She seems sure," I said, telling myself it was true.

Colton gave a cold, chopped laugh. "Well, as long as she's sure."

And then he was gone. The door banged hollowly behind him.

Max and I stared.

I thought I should apologize. Logically, I knew none of this was my fault. I'd done what any reasonable best friend would do. I'd tried to keep Brooklyn from getting swept up in short-term emotions, to make sure she considered all the ramifications of her decision.

"What about you?" Max said.

I didn't understand the question. Was he thinking the same thing I was thinking? Was he asking for an apology?

He pivoted to face me and took both of my hands in his. His touch was tender, and his gaze softened to azure. "What about us?"

Then I understood. "I can't stay." Even though, this exact moment, I was wishing with all my heart that I could.

He searched my expression for a minute. "Do you think this is something?"

I did. So help me, I did.

I'd never felt anything like this before. Max was exciting and funny, smart and thoughtful. Sex with him had been amazing with a capital *A*.

So I stood there wishing. I wished with all my heart. But I knew my weakness.

From minute one, I looked at men as potential life mates. I did it for myself and for all of my friends. In the presence of an eligible man, I went from logical mathematician to hopeless romantic.

Maybe it was my age. Anthropologically speaking, I was at a prime age to seek out a mate and have children. I took some comfort in having a logical basis for my illogical emotional reaction.

This was nothing more than anthropology.

"It's something," I said as disappointment slithered through my aching chest. "It was a wonderful weekend. Honestly, it was the best fling of my life."

He stared at me while my words hung there between us. I could only imagine he was wondering how many flings I'd had.

None was the answer. But I wasn't about to admit it. Let him think I flung, or flinged—or whatever the heck you called it—all the time. It was easier that way.

As the silent seconds ticked by, my words felt more and more like a lie.

I doubled down. "Let's not try to make it what it wasn't."

"What wasn't it?" There was a challenge in his deep, soft tone.

I was dying here. "Something serious. Something real. Something lasting."

"You're sure about that?"

I was sure. I had to be sure. I had no choice but to be sure.

I could estimate the mathematical odds of Max's and my vastly different lives meshing in any long-lasting way. Sadly for me, I could estimate them with extraordinary precision. Technically speaking, those were some very, very long odds.

Lightning hadn't struck here, even though I could swear I heard a sizzle somewhere in the middle of the night.

He reached out and tenderly stroked my hair. "Ah, Layla." He sounded sad.

I didn't exactly know what he meant. But my entire body sighed, and I only just stopped myself from leaning into his palm.

"I should go," I said.

"How long?" he asked.

My confusion must have been apparent.

"How long do we have before you go?"

"Really?" I had to admit, I was pretty startled by his request. Not unwilling, I'm embarrassed to say, but startled. "You want to hop in bed, sort of, for the road?"

Looking distinctly annoyed, he let his hand fall to his side. "Did I say that?"

"It's what you meant." I was positive on that.

He might try to walk it back, but that was exactly what he'd meant.

"I was going to suggest a chocolate soufflé." He paused. "For the road."

I tried to interpret his expression. It looked sincere. And if that was a lie, he'd thought it up awfully fast. Still...

"There's something wrong with you," he said, a trace of humor in his tone. "So skeptical."

"Are you denying you want to have sex with me?"

"I'll always want to have sex with you. But if we're talking a last memory here, I'd rather it be chocolate soufflé." He smiled. "Do you have any idea how cute you look eating chocolate soufflé?"

"I do not." I looked exactly the same eating chocolate soufflé as I did eating anything else.

"It's like you're having an orgasm right there in front of me."

"Shut up." I wasn't going to be embarrassed.

He was making this all up.

"Hot chocolate is a close second," he said. "But there's nothing like chocolate soufflé to get you going."

"You're impossible."

"You're beautiful." He gently touched beneath my chin.

"Now you're trying to distract me."

"I'm trying to change your mind. Don't go."

"Max."

"I'm serious. You don't have to leave."

"Don't do this."

It was bad enough that my brain took off on flights of fantasy about happily-ever-after. The last thing I needed was Max feeding into it.

"You know it's over," I said for both of us. "Don't pretend, not even for a little while."

I needed to stay strong. This talk of a possible future was making me even sadder than I already was.

"Why?" he asked. "Give me one good reason why we don't have a shot?"

"There's a wedding in eleven days. Brooklyn needs me. James needs me. My family is counting on me."

"This isn't about the wedding. The wedding is short-term. After—"

"No." I put my fingertips across his lips to stop him from talking.

I realized my mistake when pulses of energy shot desire into my palm and up my arm, heading for my heart.

"We're not going to recapture this," I said, much as I was thinking I would love to do that very thing. "You've got hotels to run and I've got students to teach. Brooklyn is a permanent part of my life, and Colton is a permanent part of yours."

"We can work around that."

"Listen to yourself." I was starting to feel desperate.

I took a step back.

He stared at me for a long minute.

I wanted to leave, but I couldn't seem to make my feet move.

"If you're not feeling it," he finally said.

"I'm not feeling it," I lied. I was feeling it all too strongly.

"We're not going to have that soufflé, are we?"

I shook my head. "Goodbye, Max."

His mouth tightened down to a thin line. "If that's the way you want it."

I stood my ground. "It's the way I want it."

After a moment, his eyes hardened, his gaze remote, and he took a step back—him and his perfect shaggy-neat hair and his perfect body and his perfect lovemaking.

He was writing me off, and it was physically painful.

I wanted to tell him I'd had a fantastic time, that he was an amazing man, that the reckless emotional side of me I barely knew had wanted to hang on to him and never let go.

But I'd never been one to give in to that side. And I wasn't about to start now. Right now, I had to get Brooklyn to Seattle and to the church. She'd made a brave and good decision, and I had to support her.

The sooner I turned Max into a memory, the better off I'd be.

* * *

Nat stood next to me in front of the mirrored wall in the bridal shop. It was our final bridesmaid dress fitting before the wedding on Saturday.

The dresses were light and breezy, azure-blue chiffon with knee-length hemlines. Their snug, fitted bodices with strapless sweetheart necklines were feminine and beautiful.

Nat was wearing a pretty pair of silver sandals with a satin band and two-inch heel.

I was feeling bold. I'd gone with a strappy, stylized pair with higher heels and a lot of jeweled flash.

I figured I could make it down the aisle and through the photo session without completely killing my feet. And, after that, there was a sit-down dinner that would give them a rest.

For the dancing, I'd tuck a pair of blue ballet flats into my purse. I'm not masochistic.

"You look great," I said to Nat.

It was true, but she seemed uncertain as she gazed into the mirror. Feature for feature, she was as pretty as any of us. But she never saw it, and was always doing everything she could to downplay her looks.

"You look tall," she said and put on a grin.

I was glad to see her mood shift. I knew she'd been fighting depression since Henry had dumped her. Not that Henry was a prize. Still, it was hard on a person's ego to be the one left behind.

That hadn't been the case with me and Max.

I'd been the one to make the decision that it was over.

And it was over, and it was the right decision, and I had to stop thinking about him when there were so many other things that needed my attention right now.

I put a foot forward in the reflection and turned my

ankle back and forth to make the jewels sparkle. "I couldn't resist them," I said to Nat.

"Your funeral," she answered back.

"I'm not going to dance in them or anything."

"Even without any dancing, you're going to have to last at least two hours on your feet." Nat was practical, as always.

I was practical, too. But I wasn't obsessive about it. I knew there were times when impracticality was the most practical thing to do.

"I'll be fine," I said. It would be well worth sore feet and maybe a blister or two to be immortalized in these babies in the wedding photos.

Sophie came from behind us and stood on the other side of Nat.

"We're going to knock 'em dead," Sophie said.

"That's Brooklyn's job," I pointed out, glancing to the closed curtain of the cubical where Brooklyn was slipping into her wedding dress.

She'd seemed happy since we got back from Vegas. There were times when I thought she was a little too happy. I hadn't spent as much time as I would have liked with her these past days. James was sticking close to her, and he was still giving me the cold shoulder.

I hadn't brought up his outburst in Vegas. I knew we'd have to talk it through at some point. But I'd decided it wasn't urgent.

To be fair to him, I'd mulled over the amount of time I spent with Brooklyn, trying to see it from his perspective. I had to admit we did spend a lot of time together. But it had remained steady over the years, and James had never said it was a problem.

He'd gone off about the Fuzzy Lake trips. Sure, Brooklyn and I always shared a room at Fuzzy Lake. But my parents had always been with us on the trip. We'd started going to Fuzzy Lake when we were kids. It wasn't like Brooklyn was about to sleep with James with our parents along with us.

I mean, maybe once they got into their twenties, or maybe last year when they got engaged. But nobody had suggested it. My mom had booked the rooms the same way she always did—me sharing with Brooklyn, and James sharing with our cousin Neil.

And we'd had a blast. There was no denying everyone had a blast at Fuzzy Lake.

Brooklyn and I had a standing date at a Seattle tennis club. There was that. Friday afternoons, after school was out and she left the store early, we'd play a match, then stop by the lounge for a drink. The drinks often turned into appetizers that substituted for dinner.

It wasn't like James would leave the office early. And Friday was the one day a week that Brooklyn and I truly got to touch base.

I couldn't figure out what James meant about last Christmas. Nothing out of the ordinary had happened last Christmas.

The more I thought about it, the more self-righteous I started feeling. Honestly, if James had a problem with me and Brooklyn, he should have spoken up before now. We could have talked it out. I could have given him my perspective instead of having it turn into some big thing.

Keeping it bottled up inside hadn't helped anyone.

I hadn't told Brooklyn about James's outburst, either. The wedding lead-up was running smoothly, and I didn't want to introduce a problem. Not that it was a real problem. It was just, well, weird.

I hadn't brought up Colton, either, even though I was dying to know how Brooklyn felt. If ever there was something we should be talking through, this was it. But she hadn't mentioned him at all. It was like we'd both agreed to pretend Vegas hadn't happened. It was a strategy... I supposed.

Deep down in my logical soul I knew that if mentioning Colton's name was going to mess up the wedding, the wedding should probably be messed up. But I couldn't bring myself to test it.

"Brooklyn will knock them double-dead," Sophie said, bringing me back to the present.

We all smiled at our reflections, knowing it was true. It didn't matter how much we dressed up, or what kind of shoes we wore, Brooklyn would be the most dazzling woman in the church, hands down.

Brooklyn's dressing-room curtain opened, and we all turned to look.

Her bodice was pure white lace with a V-neck and cap sleeves. It was fitted snugly to her impossibly slim waist. The silk underskirt was full and flared out, covered with a wispy sheer net that was dotted with hand-stitched lace appliqués.

Her hair was gathered at the back with a jeweled comb, a few blond wisps framing her face and fanning over the dangling white sapphire earrings that matched her elegant choker. She was upscale enough for a fashion runway.

"You're a knockout," Sophie said, stepping to one side. "Come here. Stand with us."

Nat and I moved, too, making more room for Brooklyn.

"Do you have the shoes?" I asked.

Brooklyn looked tall and elegant. And the dress looked to be exactly the right length, barely brushing the floor in a circle of lace and fanning out just a few extra inches at the back in a nod to a bridal train.

She stuck out one of her feet to show off her wedding shoe.

"Perfect," I said.

"Ouch," Nat said.

"Wimp," I said to Nat.

"You'll all be envious of me during the ceremony," Nat said.

"I don't think she'll be worried about her feet while she's saying her vows," Sophie put in.

I had to agree with Sophie on that.

If I was the one getting married, the last thing I'd be thinking about was my feet.

Max popped into my mind, fully decked out in a black tux, with a white shirt and a bow tie. He looked sexy and masculine. I could see his great hair, his smile and the crinkle of his blue eyes.

As if he was right there in front of me, he took my hand, and I could feel the wedding ring slide onto my finger, cool and smooth, a circle of gold. I lifted my face for his kiss.

Man, did I miss his kiss.

I gave myself a firm mental shake.

Marrying Max. Talk about letting my imagination run away with me again.

Max was a memory now.

"My feet," Brooklyn said, and she met my gaze in the mirror, "will be the last thing I'm thinking about."

For a second, there was something in her eyes, a brittle-edged determination that caught me off guard. But then it was gone, and I wondered if I'd imagined it.

Then I wondered if I should gather up some courage and talk to her, have a heart-to-heart, bring everything out in the open in all its ugly glory before she said her final "I do." A best friend would do that.

"Still, they'll look really great," Brooklyn continued

with a grin, giving Nat a one-armed hug. "And that's what really matters, isn't it? My feet?"

Brooklyn seemed relaxed again. She seemed genuinely happy.

Again, I felt like I was looking for problems that weren't there. I did that sometimes. I really did.

"I'll never understand that attitude," Nat said to all of us. "Sacrificing comfort for beauty."

"Beauty's fun," Sophie said.

I glanced at myself in the mirror. I was vain enough to like the way I looked, vain enough to hope any eligible men at the wedding would find me attractive.

I mean, that was what I always wanted.

But my heart really wasn't into finding a long-lost second cousin of Brooklyn's that was my age. I wasn't ready to meet another man. What I really wanted was for Max to see me in this dress, and for Max to find me attractive.

I'd tried to deny it. But denial had never been my best weapon. Reality was my best weapon. I had to confront and embrace reality and find a way to make it work for me.

The seamstress joined us, checking the fit of our dresses.

She was unhappy with Nat's waistline and Sophie's neck. So the two of them followed her across the shop for alterations.

"Do you miss him?" Brooklyn asked me, meeting my gaze in the mirror again.

"Who?"

"Max."

I was surprised that she'd asked. I was a little worried that she'd asked. Vegas truly was better left in the dust.

"No." I was determined. Fake it 'til you make it and all that.

"Liar," Brooklyn said.

I gave my bare shoulders a shrug. "There's nothing to miss. It was a thing, and then it wasn't. It ran its course."

"Is that how you remember it?"

"It's like missing a chocolate milkshake after you drank it. It was good, but it was never going to last forever." I tried for a lighter tone. "For one thing, they melt."

"Guys like Max don't melt."

"They don't last, either."

Brooklyn nodded, and then she got a faraway look in her eyes.

I couldn't stay silent anymore. "What about Colton?"

She didn't respond.

"Brooklyn?"

"Hmm?"

"Colton?"

She blinked her way back. "I made the decision to leave Colton. It was final."

I accepted that. "I made a final decision to leave Max."

"My final and your final are not the same thing."

"They're both final."

She seemed to think about that. "You know, you were right all along."

"That's what I like to hear." I kept the jokes running, afraid of letting the conversation get completely serious.

"Colton was a fantasy," Brooklyn said. "I got cold feet. But right is right, and marrying James is right."

I took heart. "That's good."

She linked her arm with mine. "But you're still allowed to miss Max. You know, in the middle of the night when you're thinking about his cut bod and the way he made you moan."

"He didn't…" I didn't know why I would deny it to Brooklyn.

I needed to be honest with her at least. It was the way

to get our relationship back on an even keel. And I desperately wanted our relationship back on an even keel.

"Fine," I said. "He was off-the-charts—as a lover, I mean."

"I knew what you meant. Nobody can take away your memories."

"That's right."

The memories were mine to keep.

"And it gives you a benchmark," Brooklyn said. "Like James gives me a benchmark."

"He does?" I was beyond heartened to hear that.

"You know he does, for honesty, integrity, kindness and hard work."

I wanted to ask about sex. Then I wanted to ask if she was madly in love with James. I opened my mouth, but chickened out.

She loved him. She definitely loved him. She always had and she always would, and that was the foundation of a good marriage, a great marriage. She and James had all the ingredients of a great marriage.

"He's funny, too," I said, instead.

"A dry wit," she agreed.

"Did you tell him…?" I struggled with the nerve to finish the question. "Anything at all?"

"I told him I'd gotten nervous."

Since Brooklyn hadn't slept with Colton, I supposed that was probably enough.

"What did he say?" I asked.

"That he was grateful I was back."

"I know he is."

"Thank you for doing it."

"For lying to James?" I realized this might be the right time to bring up his outburst.

Then again, this was probably exactly the wrong time to bring up his outburst.

"For coming after me," she said.

I liked that we were being honest again. I wanted the heart-to-heart to keep going.

"If I hadn't...would you have come back?"

"I don't know." She got the faraway look again. "I was in pretty deep. It was fun and frivolous and overwhelming. I wanted to stay in the whirlwind forever."

"That's how I felt, too. Max was a whirlwind of exhilaration. But twisters are exhausting, and they can kill you in the end."

"They are. They do," Brooklyn said. Her gaze held mine for a moment. Then she turned and took my hands. "Thank you, Layla. You kept me from making a very big mistake."

I felt a welling behind my eyes. "I'm glad. You're welcome. You can always count on me."

"I know."

Ten

Organ music rose through the church rafters and the perfume of white moonstone roses wafted through the foyer where the bridal party was gathered. The stretch limousine that had dropped us off now waited at the bottom of the sweeping concrete stairway to take the bride and groom to Briarfield Park for photos after the ceremony.

James and Brooklyn had picked the park's west gardens as a backdrop. The mottled browns and deep green would highlight Brooklyn's white dress and our pale azure.

The July weather had cooperated. If anything, it was too hot for the groomsmen in their formal suits. But the garden was shaded, which the photographer told us was perfect for the pictures.

So we had that going for us.

Brooklyn's dad, Patrick, took a stealthy peep through the doorway.

"It looks like they're ready for us," he said.

Nat, who was to be first down the aisle, moved to the edge of the doorway, still out of sight from the congregation but ready to walk as soon as she got the musical cue.

Brooklyn had chosen "A Thousand Years." I thought it was perfect. Everything about the ceremony was going to be perfect—from the music to the flowers to the vows.

We were all ready.

I gave my skirt a final swish to make sure it wasn't developing static. Then I straightened my bouquet in front of me. My sandals felt good so far, and I knew my hair was in place.

I suddenly felt Brooklyn's hand on my arm.

She squeezed hard, and I turned sharply to see what was wrong.

Her eyes were huge, and her cheeks were flushed against her pale skin.

"What?" I asked, worried the heat might be getting to her.

"Layla." There was apprehension in her voice.

"What's wrong? Are you dizzy? Do you feel faint?"

It was really hot here in the church, over eighty-five degrees outside. And I knew Brooklyn hadn't eaten anything today. I tried to remember the last time she'd even had a drink of water. As her maid of honor, I should have paid more attention.

"I can't," she said in a breathless voice.

"You can't what?"

She shook her head.

My heart started sinking fast.

She couldn't be talking about the wedding. Not now. Not *right now*.

"I'm scared," she said.

"Of what?"

Patrick arrived beside us. "Here we go. You look stunning, Brooklyn." He placed her hand on his crooked elbow.

Brooklyn looked at me for help, but I didn't know what to do. Should I say something? Should I take her aside?

"You should go, Layla," her father prompted, directing with a meaningful glance to where Nat and Sophie had moved into the open doorway.

The organist started playing "A Thousand Years."

"Brooklyn?" I asked.

This was real. This was forever. As much as I longed for her to marry James, I couldn't ignore the stark expression on her face.

Then, behind us, one of the outer church doors swung open. The double doors were wide and heavy, made of thick polished oak with black iron hinges that groaned with the effort.

A hot breeze blew in as I turned.

My heart thudded hard when I saw Max silhouetted by the sun. But it stopped abruptly when I saw it wasn't Max.

It was Colton. Colton was standing in the church doorway.

He was dressed in blue jeans and a soft blue button-down shirt. His hair was messy, and a sheen of sweat covered his forehead.

I don't know why those details seemed important. But in my brain, time had slowed—every second was an eternity.

He spotted Brooklyn and froze.

She froze, too. She grabbed my arm again. This time her grip was even tighter than before.

Patrick frowned at Colton. "Excuse me. We're about to start a wedding ceremony."

Colton broke from his pose and marched toward us.

"Brooklyn," he said.

"No," I said. "No, no." This couldn't be happening. Everything was perfect. Everything!

Brooklyn sucked in a breath. It was both a gasp and a whimper.

"What's the meaning of this?" Patrick demanded of Colton.

Colton focused on Brooklyn. "Can we talk?"

I reflexively wrapped an arm around Brooklyn.

"You can't do this," I said to Colton.

But then I saw Max.

This time it really was Max in the doorway. My heart staggered to a temporary stop.

"Please," Colton said, although his voice seemed to be far away from me now.

My arm slowly dropped to my side.

I drank in the sight of Max—the blue of his eyes, the rakish stubble of his chin, the muss of his hair and the breadth of his shoulders straining against an olive-green T-shirt. He was my every dream come to life.

"What *is this*?" Patrick bellowed. "*Who* is this?"

"Brooklyn, please." Colton was in front of her now, barely inches away.

"Don't you dare touch my daughter," Patrick said.

Max moved my way.

"You can't be here," I told him.

"I couldn't stop him," Max said, slowing in front of me. His gaze held mine. "Truth is, I wouldn't stop him. I didn't want to stop him."

Nat and Sophie were staring, openmouthed, their bouquets now dangling by their sides.

It occurred to me that the congregation could see them. The minister could see them. James could see them.

Everyone in the church would know something was wrong back here.

"This is Colton," Brooklyn said to her father.

"Who is Colton? What's he doing here? Was he invited?"

My eyes begged Max to do something. I wasn't honestly sure what I wanted him to do.

Brooklyn had been freaking out a few moments ago. She was calm now. She was focused on Colton. She was gazing up at him as if the rest of the world didn't exist.

There was no way to pretend she wanted to marry James.

It was an utter disaster, but marrying James would be an even bigger disaster.

Colton was her soul mate. Any fool could see that.

"Oh, no," I whispered under my breath.

Max was the only person who heard. "There's nothing we can do to change it."

I wished there was. I truly wished there was something I could do to fix this.

Max took my hand. "Don't even try."

"Dad—" Brooklyn said.

James burst through the doorway. "What's wrong? Is somebody hurt?"

Nat and Sophie stumbled over each other getting out of his way.

"What is *he* doing here?" James demanded.

"You know him, James?" Patrick asked.

"It's Max, Layla's..." James spotted Max holding my hand.

His gaze flew back to Colton. There was a snarl on his face and a challenging rumble in his deep tone. "Who, exactly, are you?"

"James, we have to talk," Brooklyn said.

But James's gaze didn't waver from Colton.

I squeezed Max's hand. I couldn't believe this nightmare was unfolding in front of my eyes. I wanted to say something. I wanted to do something. I wanted to help James and Brooklyn, but I had no idea how.

My parents appeared then, along with Brooklyn's mother.

"For goodness sake, *close the doors*," Patrick barked.

My dad shut the double doors behind him.

"Brooklyn," James said. "You better explain."

"Come with me," Colton said to Brooklyn.

Brooklyn didn't respond. She looked like she was in shock. She was pale, and I thought she might actually faint.

I tugged my hand from Max's and elbowed Colton out of the way. I took both of Brooklyn's hands in mine.

"Look at me," I told her. "Look at me."

She did.

"You can't decide like this."

"But—"

"You can't. Let's walk outside. Let's breathe for a minute."

She stared at me. Then the uncertainty vanished from her face and she started to smile.

I suddenly saw the girl from the jungle gym, and the beach and the floater—the one who got free milkshakes and raced me until we were exhausted.

The old Brooklyn was back.

"I love you, Layla," she said.

"I know you do. I love you, too."

"You're my best and forever friend."

"I know that, too."

She looked to James. "I'm so sorry, James. I'm *so* incredibly sorry. This is all my fault." A tear then formed in her eye. "And, Dad, please know I didn't plan for this to happen. Please forgive me."

"What is this about?" Patrick asked.

"I have to go," she said. "I'm so..."

She looked at Colton, and he reached for her, taking her arm, drawing her to him.

In seconds, his arm was protectively around her and he was spiriting her out of the church foyer onto the sidewalk.

"Come with us," Max said into my ear.

I couldn't even process the request.

My attention was on James. He'd gone from ruddy anger to a face that was pale as a ghost.

Behind him, my parents looked like they'd been blindsided, which they had. I hadn't seen that expression of confusion and disappointment on my mother's face since she caught Brooklyn and me dipping into the rum-punch bowl when we were sixteen.

I wanted to tell them Brooklyn hadn't cheated. I needed to tell them that much.

I also needed to apologize for my part in it all. I'd obviously made a mistake somewhere along the line—lots of mistakes, really.

Things would have been better if I'd left Brooklyn in Vegas. I shouldn't have tried so hard to bring her back. I should have listened to what she was trying to tell me. I shouldn't have been so selfish about wanting her for a sister-in-law.

"Let's go," Max said, taking my hand again.

I snapped it back, awash in guilt. "I can't leave."

My family was hurt. They'd been deeply wounded by Max's family. They were staring at him right now as if he was the enemy, which in many ways he was.

They felt betrayed. I'd feel betrayed if I was them. And I was the only person who could explain. Not that I had the first clue of what to say to make things better.

"It's not up to you to fix anything," Max said, seeming to read my mind.

"They're my parents. He's my brother."

"I have to go," Max said, putting a question, an invitation and a demand all into his expression at once.

"Then go," I said.

"Layla."

"Go!" I repeated.

He took a backward step, watching me as he went.

Then he took another, and another, his expression harden-
ing with each one.

My heart cried out too late.

He was already gone into the blinding sunlight.

"I know how James feels," Nat said to me.

We were on the porch at the back of my parents' house
gazing at the lights in the garden.

It was Saturday, nearly a month after the debacle of
the wedding. My parents had insisted James come out
to the friends-and-family barbecue. They thought it was
time for him to get back into circulation.

He'd kept to himself these past few weeks, angry with
me, angry with the world.

"I think I do, too," I said to Nat.

I was sad and listless, as well.

I missed Max. I missed him more than I could have ever
imagined. And with Brooklyn gone—off on the exotic and
exciting life she'd chosen that I could barely imagine—
I couldn't seem to figure out how to restart my own life
here in Seattle.

I told myself it would be better in September once
school started up again.

"You've never been dumped," Nat said.

"I…" I paused to think about it.

She was right.

I'd had breakups before, but I'd always been the one
doing the leaving.

"It was bad with Henry," she said. "I thought he might
be the one, and it sent me for a loop. But we weren't even
engaged. James was left at the altar. And he was madly
in love with Brooklyn. It doesn't get any worse than that."

I supposed it didn't.

I'd tried to be realistic with James, to talk him out of

his funk, to tell him life would be good again. It would be great again.

But I wasn't selling it.

I wasn't even sure I was feeling it.

I knew he still blamed me. He blamed me for Vegas—although I'd done my absolute best. And he blamed me for monopolizing Brooklyn for all those years. The one time I brought up his outburst, he said he never had a chance. I'd never given him a chance to be Brooklyn's soul mate.

I'd disagreed. I'd tried to explain. But he wasn't in the mood to listen.

Looking back, I wondered if I should have tried harder to see his side. After all, the breakup was about him. It wasn't about me.

"Funny," I said to Nat.

"What could possibly be funny?"

"I made the same mistake with James as I did with Brooklyn. I spent all that time trying to talk her out of her emotions. I was so focused on the logic of her marrying James that I ignored the fact that she wasn't in love with him."

"You're a math teacher," Nat said. "It's your job to be unemotional."

I supposed that was true. I mean, maybe it was true.

"I wonder if it's causation or correlation," I mused out loud.

"Huh?"

"Do you suppose being a math teacher makes me unemotional? Or did I end up being a math teacher because I was already unemotional?"

"Does it matter?"

"I'm not sure. But I'm trying to understand myself."

"Why?"

"Because I'm making a lot of mistakes."

As I said the words, I realized they were true. They were at the core of my funk.

I was making mistakes and losing confidence in myself. I'd always been rock-solid in my convictions, convinced that solid logic kept you on the right path, and that I had solid logic. Emotions merely got in the way of good judgment.

"That doesn't sound like you."

My phone pinged with a text message for me.

I automatically glanced at it and was surprised to see Brooklyn's name.

I'd felt too guilty to talk to her right after the canceled wedding, feeling like I owed loyalty to my family. She'd seemed to respect the difficult situation, keeping her distance.

I sure missed her.

"It's Brooklyn," I said to Nat.

Nat sat up straighter. "Has she been staying in contact?"

I shook my head. "No."

"Me, neither," Nat said. "It was a crappy thing she did. And I didn't really know what to say."

"Are you angry?" I hadn't thought about Nat or Sophie being angry at Brooklyn.

"A little. I mean, I still love Brooklyn, but she's always been this beautiful windstorm of a person, swirling through life with the world laid out in front of her, oblivious to the destruction she's left behind."

I blinked at Nat. I didn't know what to say.

I supposed it was true, at least on some level. But it wasn't Brooklyn's fault that the world treated her like a goddess. She could have taken way more advantage than she did. Considering the sycophantic men that sought her out, I always thought she stayed pretty grounded.

"I'm sorry," Nat said. "I sounded like a witch there."

"Don't be sorry," I said. "You're not completely wrong. I just think—at least on balance—she did the best she could."

Nat nodded to the phone. "You should check to see what she said."

I was dying of curiosity, so I picked up my phone from the low table in front of me.

Her message came as a shock.

"What?" Nat prompted.

"She wants me to come to San Francisco."

"To stay for free at her new boyfriend's opulent hotel?" There was a trace of sarcasm to Nat's tone.

"No. I mean, well, probably that, too. She wants me to stand up for her when she gets married to Colton."

James's voice startled me. "You have got to be joking."

Both Nat and I turned to see James walk onto the porch. "Just like that? That fast? She's going to take up with the jerk?"

"He's not—" I stopped myself.

"It does seem awfully fast," Nat said.

James plopped down in a chair across from us. "I dated her for eight years—*eight* years. We were engaged for more than a year. And she makes a decision this fast? How does that work?"

"I won't go," I said.

"Of course you won't go," Nat said.

"You should go," James said in an irritated tone.

"I'm not going to do that to you." Even as my left brain made that perfectly reasonable logical decision, my right brain zeroed in on Max.

If I went to Brooklyn's wedding, I'd see Max. I'd love to see Max. I'd honestly give almost anything to see Max— even if he was angry, which he most certainly was.

He hadn't tried to contact me at all since the wedding.

I wanted to be mad at him for that.

I wasn't mad.

I didn't know how I felt—which was the crux of my problem.

"She's your best friend," James said.

I didn't argue that point. It was empirically true.

He drummed his fingertips on the arm of the chair. "She's been your best friend since you were, what, six years old?"

"They met at my birthday party," Nat said. She looked at me, and there was a wistful look in her eyes. "I never knew why you didn't end up as my best friend."

I felt a lurch of guilt. The emotion was strong. I realized in that moment how pivotal emotion had been to the makeup of our friendships.

I'd never thought about it before. I'd never analyzed it. Brooklyn and I just clicked.

Nat was a perfectly wonderful friend, and I adored her. But there was some kind of inner magic with Brooklyn. I felt happy just being around her.

"If you don't go, you won't forgive yourself," James said to me.

"It doesn't feel right," I said.

Wow—another emotion pushing me to make a decision. I was losing it.

Logic told me I was Brooklyn's best friend. Best friends went to each other's weddings. James was hurt, but it wasn't Brooklyn's fault. If she wasn't in love with him, she wasn't in love with him. It was marrying him under those circumstances that would have been the worst wrong.

"You have to go," James said.

I looked to Nat.

She gave a shrug. "It's Brooklyn. And you're part of the world that falls in line for her."

James looked surprised by Nat's words.

But Nat didn't look annoyed. She looked accepting.

Nat was right. James was right. Logic was right.

"I'll go," I said.

I closed my eyes for a brief second and Max's image came up behind my eyelids.

He didn't enter into the equation. I was positive on that. I knew I'd never be selfish enough to use Brooklyn as an excuse to see Max.

But then the image sharpened inside my mind, along with a wave of scents and sounds and tactile memories. The thought of Max brought such a wave of joy and anticipation that I had to wonder if I'd finally mastered the art of denial.

Brooklyn met me at the San Francisco airport.

I'd worried on the plane that it would be awkward. But we hugged, and it felt perfectly natural.

When she drew back, her smile was as ordinary as ever.

"Good flight?" she asked.

It had been a fantastic flight. "You didn't have to fly me first class."

Between the first-class lounge, preboarding, the big comfy seat and a mimosa with breakfast, I couldn't have been more spoiled.

"Colton insisted," she said.

"Quit trying to make me like him."

"Oh, you're going to like him all right. I can guarantee it."

"Bold," I said. "He can't buy my love."

Brooklyn flashed a really big diamond ring. "He bought mine."

"Yowza," I said. And I meant it.

I held her hand still and stared at the multicarat solitaire in a swirl of gold. The big stone was flanked on each side by two small emeralds. It was nontraditional, and it suited her.

"Let's go grab your bag," she said. "I've got a driver waiting."

"A driver? Like in a suit and a cap?"

She seemed to ponder that as we started walking. "I don't think he had a cap."

"Is that how you live now?" I fell into step in the crowded concourse. "Big diamonds and luxury sedans?"

"It's not like that."

I realized too late that I sounded judgmental. I didn't want to be judgmental. I wasn't judgmental. And I wasn't jealous.

At least I wasn't jealous of Brooklyn's new wealthy status. I might have been jealous of her happiness.

She looked really happy. And that made me think Colton must not be all that bad.

Brooklyn could have had James. And James was quite a catch. So if Colton was better than James, then he had to have something going for him.

If he was anything like his twin brother, he had quite a lot going for him.

I was going to see Max today.

I was going to see Max…

"Layla?" Brooklyn's voice sounded hesitant.

"What?" I gave her my full attention.

"I haven't changed."

"I know you haven't changed." I linked my arm with hers.

"Not really," she said. "Not how it counts."

"You quit your job?" I thought that was an easy assumption.

"I did."

"What will you do here, or in Vegas, or, you know, everywhere. You can't go to the spa every day."

"I'm not going to the spa every day. I might go every week. It's free for me now. Free for you this weekend, too."

"I don't think I'll be going to the spa." That wasn't where my head was at, at all.

"You can," she said.

"What are you going to do?" Now that we were talking about it, I was pretty curious about what rich people did all day.

"The Kendrick hotels have boutiques. I'm still going to be a fashion buyer, and maybe some other things, too."

"They had an opening?" I was willing to bet the owner's wife got a job whether there was an opening or not.

"I know what you're thinking."

"It's a valid thought."

"I expect they've created a special position for me for now. And everyone's going to think I'm a dilettante. And they'll probably hate me."

Her assessment seemed accurate. Although, I didn't think anyone had ever hated Brooklyn in her life. I wasn't sure how she'd cope with that.

"I'm going to have to prove myself. I'm prepared for that."

"You're prepared for people not to like you."

"I'll win them over," she said.

I believed her. And I was feeling proud of her for throwing herself into an uncomfortable situation. She could have simply gone to the spa and shopping every day. I doubted Colton would have minded.

We skirted a family pushing a huge luggage cart.

"Speaking of hating me..." she said.

"James?" I guessed.

"Is he doing okay?"

"He's getting there."

"Honestly?"

"Honestly, I think it's going to take a while. He is back to work. And he's playing tennis on Saturdays. And he did tell me to come here to be with you."

"I'm glad you came," she said.

"So am I."

Brooklyn pointed. "Carousel three. That guy there is our driver. He'll get your bag."

"It's blue and silver," I said.

"Like I won't recognize it."

Of course she'd recognize it. She was with me when I bought it. I felt silly having described it.

"I'm still me," Brooklyn said.

"I know that."

She sobered. "I didn't have a choice."

"I know that, too. I'm sorry, Brooklyn."

She looked puzzled.

"I'm sorry I pushed so hard for you to walk away from Colton. I was wrong to do that. You knew what you wanted, and I wouldn't let you tell me how sure you were."

"I wasn't sure," she said. "I got scared. I took the easy path. Marrying James was the easy path."

"It didn't end up as the easy path." I spotted my suitcase. "There it is."

Brooklyn signaled the driver and pointed to my bag.

"I try not to think about that day," she said.

I understood that. "All those guests, the flowers, the dresses. All that food."

Brooklyn looked puzzled again. "Oh, yeah."

"What were you thinking?" I asked.

"Nothing."

"Come on. Give."

She didn't answer.

"This is me," I said.

She pursed her lips, then her tone changed. "I was thinking I almost let Colton go. And that terrifies me."

Something shifted in my stomach—a burst of fear and regret.

I had let Max go that day. I sure didn't like to linger over that. When I thought about it, all I saw was the disappointment on his face, the disappointment that turned to anger as he had backed away.

Eleven

Colton's parents, David and Susan Kendrick, were gracious and welcoming. Colton was cordial, clearly giving me space. Brooklyn's parents seemed tense and uncomfortable. But they were there to support her. I admired that.

There wouldn't be a church or a walk down the aisle this time. The intimate ceremony was to take place in the Kendricks' private villa at the top of the Archway Hotel.

It was a magnificent suite with high ceilings, soaring windows and an expansive concrete patio where we'd all have a wedding dinner later on.

I was struck by the difference between this wedding and the one we'd spent a full year planning. Brooklyn had changed into a V-neck, tea-length ivory dress with a lace-covered bodice and see-through lace three-quarter-length sleeves with a full, flowing chiffon skirt. It was pretty, but hardly dramatic.

I had gone with an off-the-shoulder, teal-green satin. It had a beaded front and an asymmetrical hemline that dropped at the back. My hair was half-up, while Brooklyn's flowed in smooth waves over her shoulders.

It was clear I was more extravagantly dressed than the bride, but nobody seemed to care.

We were sipping champagne and making small talk while the hotel catering staff arranged a table and some flowers in front of the windows that overlooked the bay. A female reverend wearing a lovely cream-colored stole was lighting some candles on the small table.

The bell sounded in the villa, and what I guessed to be a butler opened the door.

I held my breath, waiting to see if it was Max.

It was, and energy rushed through me at the sight of him.

He was in a black suit, not a tux. But the effect was the same.

He looked sophisticated, handsome and confident, in his prime and at the helm of his world.

Then I saw there was a woman beside him—a beautiful blonde woman in a strapless burgundy cocktail dress. A wide band with ornate silver beading glittered beneath her bust. The two-layered skirt landed a few inches above her knees.

It was a perfect dress for dancing. And she was the perfect date for Max.

"Max, Ellen," Susan called out. "You're right on time. Come and say hello to Brooklyn's best friend, Layla."

Susan seemed to know Ellen. She seemed to know her quite well.

I felt like a fool. I'd been pining away for Max, assuming I'd angered him or hurt him, maybe even broke his heart by not leaving with him from the church that day.

Instead, here he was out on the circuit again. Or maybe she was an old girlfriend. Maybe they'd reunited. That would explain Susan's friendliness.

Whatever it was, I was totally in Max's rearview mirror.

I was never going to learn.

I took a long swig of my champagne, pulling my attention from Max and vowing not to look at him again until this was all over.

"Are we ready then?" asked the reverend.

"I'm more than ready," Colton said, and he took Brooklyn's hand.

She looked relaxed and happy—glowing like a bride should be glowing.

I took my place beside her.

Max or no Max, I was going to spend the rest of the evening being happy for Brooklyn. She deserved it.

The sun was dipping down as the reverend spoke of love, respect and commitment.

The clouds turned pink while Brooklyn and Colton said their vows.

I keep my attention firmly focused on the happy couple and the wonderful view.

Max might as well have not been there.

Except that he was there.

And I knew he was there.

I might not have been looking at him, but I was aware of his energy with every fiber of my being.

I wished my being wouldn't do that.

I wished with all my heart that I could ignore him standing there, and that I could ignore Ellen sitting behind him on the French provincial chair next to Susan and David.

Max had a girlfriend.

Short weeks ago in Vegas he'd asked me to see where our relationship might go.

I'd said no, and he'd bounced back in a heartbeat.

By the time Colton kissed the bride, I was angry with Max, and I wondered what I'd ever seen in a man so shallow.

I was mad at myself, too. I had a flawed gene or something. Eligible men made my brain turn to mush. And this eligible man had been the worst of the worst.

I glanced his way, and caught him looking back. I was mentally catapulted into his arms, into his bed, plastered against his slick naked body, which had taken me straight to Heaven.

My skin heated and my hormones rushed to life.

Then Colton whooped, and everybody clapped.

Brooklyn was married.

When Colton let her go, I gave her a warm hug. "Congratulations. I love you."

"Thanks," she said. "I'm so glad you came."

We separated. "So am I. *So* am I."

While the photographer worked with Brooklyn and Colton, and the hotel staff set up for dinner, I found my way to the powder room.

Like everything in the villa, like everything in the entire hotel, the powder room was posh and beautifully appointed.

I wasted as much time as I could fussing with my hair, washing my hands, rubbing on some wildflower-scented lotion. I had no desire to make small talk before dinner.

When I left the powder room, I found a door that led to the far end of the patio. The patio was a crescent shape, giving me privacy.

The sun had gone down, and the lights of the harbor were coming up.

It was a serene and beautiful sight. I tried to absorb the serenity, but my nerves didn't want to calm down. They were an insistent jangle of frustration and disappointment.

I heard footsteps.

I could tell it was a man.

I willed them to go away, to stay away, to let me wallow here all by myself.

I absolutely didn't want it to be Max.

It was Max.

"Don't make this harder," I said as he stopped next to me at the rail.

"Harder than what?"

"Harder than it has to be. We don't have to talk. We don't have to interact." I kept my gaze focused on the view in front of me.

"What if I want to interact?"

I gave a chopped laugh. "I can't see why you'd want to do that. I'm the one-night stand that was forced to attend your brother's wedding."

"Nobody forced you." He sounded annoyed.

"You're right. I'm here for Brooklyn. I'll always be there for Brooklyn."

"Layla."

"Go away."

"Look at me."

"No."

He angled his body to try to get in front of my face.

I kept my gaze fixed on the view.

"Why are you being like this?" he asked.

My nerves were stretched about as far as they could go.

Max had completely and unequivocally walked away from me. He was indifferent and erratic, and all I could think was that I wanted him.

I wanted to hug him close. I wanted to kiss him. I wanted to make love with him over and over and over again.

I almost laughed. I was laughing at myself for being so out of control.

"What's funny?"

Nothing—nothing was remotely funny.

I sobered and looked him in the eyes. "What do you want from me, Max?"

"What I've always wanted from you."

"So, sex."

He frowned. "No, not sex. Why are you always talking about sex?"

"That's what we have together..." I caught myself. "I mean, that's what we had together."

"I don't want sex," he all but shouted.

Then he glanced over his shoulder toward the other end of the patio. He lowered his voice. "Of course I want sex. But I don't *only* want sex."

"Well, there is the chocolate soufflé, I suppose. But that's really only good with the sex. At least that's how I remember it. I mean, when I think about chocolate soufflé." I was babbling, but I couldn't seem to stop myself.

"Have you had too much to drink?" he asked.

"I don't believe so."

"You were there, right?"

I had no idea what he was talking about. "I was where, when?"

"In the church, at your brother's wedding, when I asked you to come away with me, to be with me, to *stay* with me."

"Did you mean for the weekend?" I asked, my own voice getting louder as I grew angry.

He opened his mouth to answer, but I didn't let him.

"How fast did you find her?" I asked. "Same day? Next day? Did you ask her to come away with you, too?"

"Who?" Max barked.

I didn't seem to care that others might be listening. I knew that was weird. But I didn't quite know how to stop it. "What do you mean, *who*?"

"It's a one-word question, Layla."

"Let me spell out a one-word answer—*E-L-L-E-N*." I thought about the spelling for a second. "At least I assume it's one *L*. That would be the normal spelling." I realized too late my dramatic answer would lose some of its oomph if I got the spelling wrong.

"Ellen?" Max asked.

"Give the man a prize."

"My cousin?"

I stilled.

My brain flatlined.

Ellen was his cousin?

"Layla," Max said, his voice echoing in my ears.

I was mortified. Now there was an emotion for you. I had absolutely no trouble feeling that one.

"I thought she was your girlfriend." There was no way I could talk myself out of this corner. The bald truth was my only option.

Max lowered his voice. "I don't have a girlfriend."

"How was I supposed to know that?"

"I was with you less than a month ago."

"You weren't exactly *with* me."

"What would you call it? And don't you dare say it was a one-night stand."

I struggled for the right words. "Well, we'd called it quits in Vegas."

"You walked away in Vegas. I came after you."

I shook my head. That wasn't exactly what had happened. "Colton came after Brooklyn. You were with him."

Max took my hand.

I knew I should pull away, but for the life of me, I didn't have the strength.

"Colton might have come after Brooklyn. But *I* came after *you*. My brother is perfectly capable of kidnapping a bride all on his own. He didn't need my help." Max paused. "I came after you, and you turned me down flat."

I remembered his expression all over again. "I..."

He waited. "You told me to go, in no uncertain terms."

He was right. I had done that.

"I didn't mean forever," I said.

This time it was Max who went still. He drew a deep breath. "It sounded like you meant forever."

"I couldn't leave my family then."

I realized I could leave them now.

It would be tough, and it would take them a while to get over it, and maybe it wasn't the smartest, most logical thing for me to do. After all, I hadn't known Max very long, and what we had might or might not last. I might be hurting my brother and my parents over something that wasn't even going to last.

But this was too important.

I was in love with Max.

It was another emotion that was perfectly clear to me. Two in one day, how about that?

"I love you," I said.

It was a stupid thing to say out loud, especially under the circumstances, and especially since he hadn't said it first, and because it laid me bare and vulnerable. But the odd thing was I didn't care.

"Not as much as I love you," he said.

My heart all but shouted with joy. I made a last-ditch fight for logic. "You can't know yours is more."

"I loved you first," he said. "That makes mine more."

"You can't know you were first."

He moved his mouth toward mine. "I don't care." He drew closer and closer.

It wasn't a contest. It wasn't—

He kissed me, and my world lit up with love and joy, excitement and hope.

It was a long time before we moved a few inches apart.

"Neither do I," I whispered to him.

"*There* you are." It was Brooklyn. "Quit ruining Layla's makeup and get in here for the pictures."

Max grinned.

"She doesn't seem surprised," I said.

"She's been with us for a month. She knows how I feel."

I gave Brooklyn a reproachful look.

She grinned like she didn't care.

Max put a hand on the small of my back, urging me toward the door.

"Some best friend you are," I said to Brooklyn.

"I didn't want to push," she said.

"*This time* you don't want to push?" Brooklyn had been talking me into outlandish things since grade school.

She turned serious. "You had to figure it out for yourself. I couldn't afford to be wrong."

I realized in that moment that she was smarter than me. I'd tried to push her in the wrong direction and nearly ruined everyone's lives.

She went ahead of us, joining Colton in the living room.

Max raised my hand to his lips and put a featherlight kiss on my knuckles.

"Now what?" I asked.

He gave a contented smile. "Now, we have dinner with my family, then wedding cake, then my suite and then chocolate soufflé."

My heart seemed to bloom inside my chest. "I do love chocolate soufflé."

When I pictured my wedding—and I'd pictured it a lot over the years—I imagined a long white dress, a flowing

train, maybe a nod to a veil, nothing covering my face, but
a bit of gauze and lace streaming from my hair. And the
flowers, I loved a wildflower bouquet: daisies and prim-
roses, violets and cornflowers. I pictured greens and colors in a messy bundle, maybe tied with ribbon instead of
arranged into a plastic handle.

It would be at St. Fidelis's, our family church, which
was big enough to hold all the friends and relatives that
would come to celebrate. I wanted a rehearsal dinner at
the tennis club—it had a magnificent view of the harbor.

And the reception, ah, the reception. There were three
possible hotels in the downtown area. I'd thought I'd tour
them and make my choice. There'd be a nice dinner, a
band, dancing and a huge cake, maybe five tiers, but not
a fruitcake. I wanted people to enjoy eating the cake. Va-
nilla pound cake, maybe, or something layered with puff
pastry, buttercream icing for sure. I absolutely adored
buttercream icing.

In all those years, in all my musings, I'd never once
pictured myself getting married in Vegas.

Don't get me wrong, an Elvis chapel might be right for
some people, but it wasn't what I had pictured. We were
set up in a wonderful corner of the atrium at the Canterbury Sands. It was tasteful and beautiful and, it turns out,
everything I really wanted in a wedding. Because all I really wanted was Max.

Brooklyn was here, but she was the only person from
my side.

I knew my eloping would upset my family. But I didn't
know how to do this without upsetting my family. A Seattle wedding, even a small one, where I married Colton's
brother would be unthinkable. A big wedding was completely out of the question.

September was coming fast, and Max and I were absolutely sure about our future. I wasn't going back to teaching at North Hill High, and I couldn't imagine telling my family I was quitting my job and moving in with Max without marrying him.

So here we were.

I'd call them later tonight and give them the good news. At least I'd act like it was good news. It was good news to me. I couldn't be happier.

We were on a small patio, near the babbling brook, beneath the palms and mesquites and amongst the cacti and wildflowers blooming in the gardens.

I'd gone with a simple white dress, knee-length, with a scooped neckline and wide shoulder straps, with just a hint of eyelet in the breezy cotton fabric. But I had my wildflower bouquet and some really awesome shoes, white and jeweled with high, high heels. I only had to stand in them for thirty minutes or so.

"When you know, you know," Brooklyn whispered to me in an I-told-you-so tone.

I'd give her that one. She had told me so.

"I know," I said back.

"I know you know," she said with a grin. "Now, look." She nodded her head.

I looked down the pathway expecting to see Max and Colton. His parents were already here, as was the reverend who had married Brooklyn and Colton.

To my surprise, I saw Nat and Sophie.

I think I gave a gasp because Brooklyn laughed at me.

"How did you…?"

"Brooklyn told us," Nat called out. "There was no way we were missing this."

"I can't believe you're here," I said to both of them.

"I can't believe you weren't going to tell us," Sophie said.

"You know it's—" I spotted James—my brother, James—coming down the pathway.

Shock didn't begin to describe my reaction. Then my reaction turned to fear.

How was he here? Why was he here? *What* was he going to do?

"Hi, Layla," he said. He sounded calm, like the old James—the James-who-wasn't-so-angry-at-me-that-he'd-never-get-over-it James.

"I don't understand." I didn't.

"Brooklyn called me," he said.

I sought out Brooklyn again, not bothering to disguise my astonishment. "*Why* would you do that?"

"They're your family," Brooklyn said.

At that very second, I saw my parents.

They were smiling, and looked for all the world as if this were a perfectly normal wedding.

My mom pulled me into a hug. "It's not your fault," she said and held me tight.

My dad hugged me next.

Then I stepped back to take in everyone.

"We're all happy for you," James said.

I watched his expression closely, not quite trusting it, worried about what would happen when Colton arrived with Max.

"Are you okay?" I asked.

His gaze slid to Brooklyn. "This is weird," he said.

"I'll say it's weird." My brain was scrambling to take it all in.

"I'll manage," he said. "And I know it's not your fault. I'm sorry I said those things."

I had to ask. "Did you really feel that way?"

James shrugged. "Sometimes. But looking back... Clearly, as they say, it wasn't you. It was me."

"I'm so sorry."

He shook his head. "Don't be. I'm fine. I'll *be* fine."

My mom reached for my hand. "This is your day, honey. Don't you worry about anything else."

Max and Colton came around the corner from Max's suite patio.

They both stopped dead and stared at my family.

Colton saw James and a muscle ticked in his cheek.

"You didn't *tell* them?" I asked Brooklyn.

"I was worried they'd be worried."

A few seconds slipped past in silence.

It was my dad who stepped up, walking toward Max and Colton, holding out his hand to Max.

"We haven't been properly introduced," he said. "I'm Al Gillen."

"Max Kendrick." Max shook his hand. His expression remained wary.

"I understand you're marrying my daughter."

"Yes, sir."

My dad looked around the garden. "I can't say this was what I was expecting."

"In a wedding?" Max asked.

"In a Vegas wedding," my dad answered. "It's nice here. It's really nice."

Max caught my gaze. He looked as confused as I felt.

"Brooklyn invited everyone," I said.

Colton's eyebrows went up, and he quickly sought out Brooklyn.

Brooklyn gave her best sparkly, love-me smile. "Everyone is happy for Layla. And everyone is happy for Max." She took my hand. "Let's do this. We can finish the introductions later."

Max was already moving to my side.

"Are you okay?" he asked as we positioned ourselves in front of the white vine-entwined arch.

"I'm pretty stunned," I said.

"And your brother?"

I gave a glance to James. He was staying well away from Colton, but otherwise he looked like he was handling it.

"It must have been his decision to come."

Max squeezed my hand. "I'm glad. I'm really glad your family is here."

"So am I." For a second I had to fight a tear of joy.

"They love you," Max said. "And I love you."

"This is a good beginning," I said, facing the reverend, seeing my life with Max flowing out like a pathway in front of me.

Brooklyn would be in our lives, and Colton would be in our lives, and our families would be there to support us.

In time, James's broken heart would heal. This was the start of that, too.

"Family and friends," the reverend began. "We're gathered here to celebrate a day of happiness."

Max put an arm around me and pulled me to him.

I rested my head on his shoulder, feeling his steadiness and strength, knowing deep in my soul my decision was right. Our happiness was going to last forever.

* * * * *

*Don't miss Nat's big romance
coming in March from award-winning author
Barbara Dunlop and Harlequin Desire!*

*For more great titles from Barbara Dunlop,
go to www.Harlequin.com today!*

COMING NEXT MONTH FROM

DESIRE

Available February 4, 2020

#2713 FROM BOARDROOM TO BEDROOM
Texas Cattleman's Club: Inheritance • by Jules Bennett
Sophie Blackwood needs the truth to take back what rightfully belongs to her family. Working for media CEO Nigel Townshend is the way to do it. What she doesn't expect is their undeniable attraction. Will her feelings for her British playboy boss derail everything?

#2714 BLAME IT ON THE BILLIONAIRE
Blackout Billionaires • by Naima Simone
Nadia Jordan certainly didn't plan on spending the night with Grayson Chandler during the blackout, but the bigger surprise comes when he introduces her as his fake fiancée to avoid his family's matchmaking! But even a fake relationship can't hide their real chemistry...

#2715 RULE BREAKER
Dynasties: Mesa Falls • by Joanne Rock
Despite his bad-boy persona, Mesa Falls ranch owner Weston Rivera takes his job very seriously—a point he makes clear to meddlesome financial investigator April Stephens. Stranded together by a storm, their attraction is searing, but can it withstand their differences once the snow clears?

#2716 ONE LITTLE INDISCRETION
Murphy International • by Joss Wood
After their night of passion, auction house CEO Carrick Murphy and art detective Sadie Slade aren't looking for anything more. But when she learns she's pregnant, they must overcome their troubled pasts for a chance at lasting happiness...

#2717 HIS FORBIDDEN KISS
Kiss and Tell • by Jessica Lemmon
Heiress Taylor Thompson never imagined her night would end with kissing a mysterious stranger—let alone her reluctant date's older brother, Royce Knox! Their spark can't be denied, but will family and professional pressure keep them to just one kiss?

#2718 TEMPORARY WIFE TEMPTATION
The Heirs of Hansol • by Jayci Lee
To keep his role as CEO, Garrett Song needs to find a bride, and fast. And Natalie Sobol is the perfect candidate. But their marriage of convenience is rocked when real passion takes over. Can a bargain that was only supposed to be temporary last forever?
